Farm

The Dragon

"Excuse me," said the dragon, "but were you looking for me by any chance?"

"No, indeed!" said the farmer. "Who'd a' thought of seeing you here? I was just going for a ride."

★ ★ ★ ★

"As you like," said Chrysophylax, licking his lips again, but pretending to close his eyes. He had a wicked heart (as all dragons have), but not a very bold one (as is not unusual). He preferred a meal that he did not have to fight for; but appetite had returned after a good long sleep. The parson of Oakley had been stringy, and it was years since he had tasted a large fat man. He now had made up his mind to try this easy meat, and he was only waiting until the old fool was off his guard.

But the old fool was not as foolish as he looked . . .

Works by J.R.R. Tolkien

The Hobbit*
Leaf by Niggle
On Fairy-Stories
Farmer Giles of Ham*
The Homecoming of Beorhtnoth
The Lord of the Rings*
The Adventures of Tom Bombadil
The Road Goes Ever On (*with Donald Swann*)
Smith of Wootton Major*

Works Published Posthumously
Sir Gawain and the Green Knight, Pearl, and Sir Orfeo*
The Father Christmas Letters
The Silmarillion*
Pictures by J.R.R. Tolkien
Unfinished Tales*
The Letters of J.R.R. Tolkien
Finn and Hingest
Mr. Bliss
The Monsters and the Critics & Other Essays
Roverandom
The Children of Húrin*
The Legend of Sigurd and Gudrún
The Fall of Arthur

The History of Middle-earth
I. The Book of Lost Tales, Part One*
II. The Book of Lost Tales, Part Two*
III. The Lays of Beleriand*
IV. The Shaping of Middle-earth*
V. The Lost Road and Other Writings*
VI. The Return of the Shadow
VII. The Treason of Isengard
VIII. The War of the Ring
IX. Sauron Defeated
X. Morgoth's Ring
XI. The War of the Jewels
XII. The Peoples of Middle-earth

Adapted by Charles Dixon with Sean Deming:
The Hobbit: An Illustrated Edition*

By Robert Foster:
The Complete Guide to Middle-earth*

*Published by The Random House Publishing Group

J.R.R. TOLKIEN

SMITH OF WOOTTON MAJOR

FARMER GILES OF HAM

Illustrations
by
Pauline Diana Baynes

A Del Rey ® Book
BALLANTINE BOOKS • NEW YORK

A Del Rey® Book
Published by The Random House Publishing Group

Published in the United States by Del Rey Books, an imprint of The Random House Publishing Group, a division of Random House, Inc., New York.

DEL REY is a registered trademark and the Del Rey colophon is a trademark of Random House, Inc.

ISBN 978-0-345-33606-4

This edition published by arrangement with Houghton Mifflin Company

Printed in the United States of America

www.delreybooks.com

First Ballantine Books Edition: March 1969

Contents

Smith
of Wootton Major

THERE was a village once, not very long ago for those with long memories, nor very far away for those with long legs. Wootton Major it was called because it was larger than Wootton Minor, a few miles away deep in the trees; but it was not very large, though it was at that time prosperous, and a fair number of folk lived in it, good, bad, and mixed, as is usual.

It was a remarkable village in its way, being well known in the country round about for the skill of its workers in various crafts, but most of all for its cooking. It had a large Kitchen which belonged to the Village Council, and the Master Cook was an important person. The Cook's House and the Kitchen adjoined the Great Hall, the largest and oldest building in the place and the most beautiful. It was built of good stone and good oak and was

well tended, though it was no longer painted or
gilded as it had been once upon a time. In the
Hall the villagers held their meetings and debates,
and their public feasts, and their family gatherings.
So the Cook was kept busy, since for all these occasions he had to provide suitable fare. For the
festivals, of which there were many in the course
of a year, the fare that was thought suitable was
plentiful and rich.

There was one festival to which all looked forward, for it was the only one held in winter. It
went on for a week, and on its last day at sundown
there was a merrymaking called The Feast of
Good Children, to which not many were invited.
No doubt some who deserved to be asked were
overlooked, and some who did not were invited by
mistake; for that is the way of things, however
careful those who arrange such matters may try to
be. In any case it was largely by chance of birthday
that any child came in for the Twenty-four Feast,
since that was only held once in twenty-four years,
and only twenty-four children were invited. For
that occasion the Master Cook was expected to do
his best, and in addition to many other good things
it was the custom for him to make the Great Cake.
By the excellence (or otherwise) of this his name
was chiefly remembered, for a Master Cook seldom
if ever lasted long enough in office to make a second
Great Cake.

There came a time, however, when the reigning Master Cook, to everyone's surprise, since it had never happened before, suddenly announced that he needed a holiday; and he went away, no one knew where; and when he came back some months later he seemed rather changed. He had been a kind man who liked to see other people enjoying themselves, but he was himself serious, and said very little. Now he was merrier, and often said and did most laughable things; and at feasts he would himself sing gay songs, which was not expected of Master Cooks. Also he brought back with him an apprentice; and that astonished the village.

It was not astonishing for the Master Cook to have an apprentice. It was usual. The Master chose one in due time, and he taught him all that he could; and as they both grew older the apprentice took on more of the important work, so that when the Master retired or died there he was, ready to take over the office and become Master Cook in his turn. But this Master had never chosen an apprentice. He had always said "time enough yet," or "I'm keeping my eyes open and I'll choose one when I find one to suit me." But now he brought with him a mere boy, and not one from the village. He was more lithe than the Wootton lads and quicker, soft-spoken and very polite, but ridiculously young for the work, barely in his teens by the look of him. Still, choosing his apprentice was the Master Cook's affair, and no one had the right to interfere in it; so the boy remained and stayed in the Cook's House until he was old enough to find lodgings for himself. People soon became used to seeing him about, and he made a few friends. They and the Cook called him Alf, but to the rest he was just Prentice.

The next surprise came only three years later. One spring morning the Master Cook took off his tall white hat, folded up his clean aprons, hung up his white coat, took a stout ash stick and a small bag, and departed. He said goodbye to the apprentice. No one else was about.

"Goodbye for now, Alf," he said. "I leave you to manage things as best you can, which is always very well. I expect it will turn out all right. If we meet again, I hope to hear all about it. Tell them that I've gone on another holiday, but this time I shan't be coming back again."

There was quite a stir in the village when Prentice gave this message to people who came to the Kitchen. "What a thing to do!" they said. "And without warning or farewell! What are we going to do without any Master Cook? He has left no one to take his place." In all their discussions no one ever thought of making young Prentice into Cook.

He had grown a bit taller but still looked like a boy, and he had only served for three years.

In the end for lack of anyone better they appointed a man of the village, who could cook well enough in a small way. When he was younger he had helped the Master at busy times, but the Master had never taken to him and would not have him as apprentice. He was now a solid sort of man with a wife and children, and careful with money. "At any rate he won't go off without notice," they said, "and poor cooking is better than none. It is seven years till the next Great Cake, and by that time he should be able to manage it."

Nokes, for that was his name, was very pleased with the turn things had taken. He had always wished to become Master Cook, and had never doubted that he could manage it. For some time, when he was alone in the Kitchen, he used to put on the tall white hat and look at himself in a polished frying pan and say: "How do you do, Master. That hat suits you properly, might have been made for you. I hope things go well with you."

Things went well enough; for at first Nokes did his best, and he had Prentice to help him. Indeed he learned a lot from him by watching him slyly, though that Nokes never admitted. But in due course the time for the Twenty-four Feast drew near, and Nokes had to think about making the Great Cake. Secretly he was worried about it, for although with seven years' practice he could turn out passable cakes and pastries for ordinary occasions, he knew that his Great Cake would be eagerly awaited, and would have to satisfy severe critics. Not only the children. A smaller cake of the same materials and baking had to be provided for those who came to help at the feast. Also it was expected that the Great Cake should have something novel and surprising about it and not be a mere repetition of the one before.

His chief notion was that it should be very sweet and rich; and he decided that it should be entirely covered in sugar-icing (at which Prentice had a clever hand). "That will make it pretty and fairylike," he thought. Fairies and sweets were two of the very few notions he had about the tastes of children. Fairies he thought one grew out of; but of sweets he remained very fond. "Ah! fairylike," he said, "that gives me an idea"; and so it came into his head that he would stick a little doll on a pinnacle in the middle of the Cake, dressed all in white, with a little wand in her hand ending in a tinsel star, and *Fairy Queen* written in pink icing round her feet.

But when he began preparing the materials for the cake-making he found that he had only dim memories of what should go *inside* a Great Cake;

so he looked in some old books of recipes left behind by previous cooks. They puzzled him, even when he could make out their handwriting, for they mentioned many things that he had not heard of, and some that he had forgotten and now had no time to get; but he thought he might try one or two of the spices that the books spoke of. He scratched his head and remembered an old black box with several different compartments in which the last Cook had once kept spices and other things for special cakes. He had not looked at it since he took over, but after a search he found it on a high shelf in the store-room.

He took it down and blew the dust off the lid; but when he opened it he found that very little of the spices was left, and they were dry and musty. But in one compartment in the corner he discovered a small star, hardly as big as one of our sixpences, black-looking as if it was made of silver but was tarnished. "That's funny!" he said as he held it up to the light.

"No, it isn't!" said a voice behind him, so suddenly that he jumped. It was the voice of Prentice, and he had never spoken to the Master in that tone before. Indeed he seldom spoke to Nokes at all unless he was spoken to first. Very right and proper in a youngster; he might be clever with icing but he had a lot to learn yet: that was Nokes's opinion.

"What do you mean, young fellow?" he said, not much pleased. "If it isn't funny what is it?"

"It is *fay*," said Prentice. "It comes from Faery."

Then the Cook laughed. "All right, all right," he said. "It means much the same; but call it that if you like. You'll grow up some day. Now you can get on with stoning the raisins. If you notice any funny fairy ones, tell me."

"What are you going to do with the star, Master?" said Prentice.

"Put it into the Cake, of course," said the Cook. "Just the thing, especially if it's *fairy*," he sniggered. "I daresay you've been to children's parties yourself, and not so long ago either, where little trinkets like this were stirred into the mixture, and little coins and what not. Anyway we do that in this village: it amuses the children."

"But this isn't a trinket, Master, it's a fay-star," said Prentice.

"So you've said already," snapped the Cook. "Very well, I'll tell the children. It'll make them laugh."

"I don't think it will, Master," said Prentice. "But it's the right thing to do, quite right."

"Who do you think you're talking to?" said Nokes.

In time the Cake was made and baked and iced, mostly by Prentice. "As you are so set on fairies,

I'll let you make the Fairy Queen," Nokes said to him.

"Very good, Master," he answered. "I'll do it if you are too busy. But it was your idea and not mine."

"It's my place to have ideas, and not yours," said Nokes.

At the Feast the Cake stood in the middle of the long table, inside a ring of twenty-four red candles. Its top rose into a small white mountain, up the sides of which grew little trees glittering as if with frost; on its summit stood a tiny white figure on one foot like a snow-maiden dancing, and in her hand was a minute wand of ice sparkling with light.

The children looked at it with wide eyes, and one or two clapped their hands, crying: "Isn't it pretty and fairylike!" That delighted the Cook, but the apprentice looked displeased. They were both present: the Master to cut up the Cake when the time came, and the apprentice to sharpen the knife and hand it to him.

At last the Cook took the knife and stepped up to the table. "I should tell you, my dears," he said, "that inside this lovely icing there is a cake made of many nice things to eat; but also stirred well in there are many pretty little things, trinkets and little coins and what not, and I'm told that it

is lucky to find one in your slice. There are twenty-four in the Cake, so there should be one for each of you, if the Fairy Queen plays fair. But she doesn't always do so: she's a tricky little creature. You ask Mr. Prentice." The apprentice turned away and studied the faces of the children.

"No! I'm forgetting," said the Cook. "There's twenty-five this evening. There's also a little silver star, a special magic one, or so Mr. Prentice says. So be careful! If you break one of your pretty front teeth on it, the magic star won't mend it. But I expect it's a specially lucky thing to find, all the same."

It was a good cake, and no one had any fault to find with it, except that it was no bigger than was needed. When it was all cut up there was a large slice for each of the children, but nothing left over: no coming again. The slices soon disappeared, and every now and then a trinket or a coin was discovered. Some found one, and some found two, and several found none; for that is the way luck goes, whether there is a doll with a wand on the cake or not. But when the Cake was all eaten, there was no sign of any magic star.

"Bless me!" said the Cook. "Then it can't have been made of silver after all; it must have melted. Or perhaps Mr. Prentice was right and it was really magical, and it's just vanished and gone back to Fairyland. Not a nice trick to play, I don't think."

He looked at Prentice with a smirk, and Prentice looked at him with dark eyes and did not smile at all.

All the same, the silver star was indeed a fay-star: the apprentice was not one to make mistakes about things of that sort. What had happened was that one of the boys at the Feast had swallowed it without ever noticing it, although he had found a silver coin in his slice and had given it to Nell, the little girl next to him: she looked so disappointed at finding nothing lucky in hers. He sometimes wondered what had really become of the star, and did not know that it had remained with him, tucked away in some place where it could not be felt; for that was what it was intended to do. There it waited for a long time, until its day came.

The Feast had been in mid-winter, but it was now June, and the night was hardly dark at all. The boy got up before dawn, for he did not wish to sleep: it was his tenth birthday. He looked out of the window, and the world seemed quiet and expectant. A little breeze, cool and fragrant, stirred the waking trees. Then the dawn came, and far away he heard the dawn-song of the birds beginning, growing as it came towards him, until it rushed over him, filling all the land round the house, and passed on like a wave of music into the West, as the sun rose above the rim of the world.

"It reminds me of Faery," he heard himself say; "but in Faery the people sing too." Then he began to sing, high and clear, in strange words that he seemed to know by heart; and in that moment the star fell out of his mouth and he caught it on his open hand. It was bright silver now, glistening in the sunlight; but it quivered and rose a little, as if it was about to fly away. Without thinking he clapped his hand to his head, and there the star stayed in the middle of his forehead, and he wore it for many years.

Few people in the village noticed it though it was not invisible to attentive eyes; but it became part of his face, and it did not usually shine at all. Some of its light passed into his eyes; and his voice, which had begun to grow beautiful as soon as the star came to him, became ever more beautiful as he grew up. People liked to hear him speak, even if it was no more than a "good morning."

He became well known in his country, not only in his own village but in many others round about, for his good workmanship. His father was a smith, and he followed him in his craft and bettered it. Smithson he was called while his father was still alive, and then just Smith. For by that time he was the best smith between Far Easton and the Westwood, and he could make all kinds of things of iron in his smithy. Most of them, of course, were plain and useful, meant for daily needs: farm tools, carpenters' tools, kitchen tools and pots and pans, bars and bolts and hinges, pot-hooks, fire-dogs, and horse-shoes, and the like. They were strong and lasting, but they also had a grace about them, being shapely in their kinds, good to handle and to look at.

But some things, when he had time, he made for delight; and they were beautiful, for he could work iron into wonderful forms that looked as light and delicate as a spray of leaves and blossom, but kept the stern strength of iron, or seemed even stronger. Few could pass by one of the gates or lattices that he made without stopping to admire it; no one could pass through it once it was shut. He sang when he was making things of this sort; and when Smith began to sing those nearby stopped their own work and came to the smithy to listen.

That was all that most people knew about him. It was enough indeed and more than most men and women in the village achieved, even those who were skilled and hard-working. But there was more to know. For Smith became acquainted with Faery, and some regions of it he knew as well as any mortal can; though since too many had become like Nokes, he spoke of this to few people, except his wife and his children. His wife was

Nell, to whom he gave the silver coin, and his daughter was Nan, and his son was Ned Smithson. From them it could not have been kept secret anyway, for they sometimes saw the star shining on his forehead, when he came back from one of the long walks he would take alone now and then in the evening, or when he returned from a journey.

From time to time he would go off, sometimes walking, sometimes riding, and it was generally supposed that it was on business; and sometimes it was, and sometimes it was not. At any rate not to get orders for work, or to buy pig-iron and charcoal and other supplies, though he attended to such things with care and knew how to turn an honest penny into twopence, as the saying went. But he had business of its own kind in Faery, and he was welcome there; for the star shone bright on his brow, and he was as safe as a mortal can be in that perilous country. The Lesser Evils avoided the star, and from the Greater Evils he was guarded.

For that he was grateful, for he soon became wise and understood that the marvels of Faery cannot be approached without danger, and that many of the Evils cannot be challenged without weapons of power too great for any mortal to wield. He remained a learner and explorer, not a warrior; and though in time he could have forged weapons that in his own world would have had power enough to become the matter of great tales

and be worth a king's ransom, he knew that in Faery they would have been of small account. So among all the things that he made it is not remembered that he ever forged a sword or a spear or an arrow-head.

In Faery at first he walked for the most part quietly among the lesser folk and the gentler creatures in the woods and meads of fair valleys, and by the bright waters in which at night strange stars shone and at dawn the gleaming peaks of far mountains were mirrored. Some of his briefer visits he spent looking only at one tree or one flower; but later in longer journeys he had seen things of both beauty and terror that he could not clearly remember nor report to his friends, though he knew that they dwelt deep in his heart. But some things he did not forget, and they remained in his mind as wonders and mysteries that he often recalled.

When he first began to walk far without a guide he thought he would discover the further bounds of the land; but great mountains rose before him, and going by long ways round about them he came at last to a desolate shore. He stood beside the Sea of Windless Storm where the blue waves like snow-clad hills roll silently out of Unlight to the long strand, bearing the white ships that return from battles on the Dark Marches of which men know nothing. He saw a great ship cast high upon

the land, and the waters fell back in foam without a sound. The eleven mariners were tall and
terrible; their swords shone and their spears glinted
and a piercing light was in their eyes. Suddenly
they lifted up their voices in a song of triumph,
and his heart was shaken with fear, and he fell
upon his face, and they passed over him and went
away into the echoing hills.

Afterwards he went no more to that strand, be-
lieving that he was in an island realm beleaguered
by the Sea, and he turned his mind towards the
mountains, desiring to come to the heart of the
kingdom. Once in these wanderings he was over-
taken by a grey mist and strayed long at a loss.
until the mist rolled away and he found that he
was in a wide plain. Far off there was a great hill
of shadow, and out of that shadow, which was its
root, he saw the King's Tree springing up, tower
upon tower, into the sky, and its light was like the
sun at noon; and it bore at once leaves and flowers
and fruits uncounted, and not one was the same
as any other that grew on the Tree.

He never saw that Tree again, though he often
sought for it. On one such journey climbing into
the Outer Mountains he came to a deep dale
among them, and at its bottom lay a lake, calm and
unruffled though a breeze stirred the woods that

surrounded it. In that dale the light was like a red sunset, but the light came up from the lake. From a low cliff that overhung it he looked down, and it seemed that he could see to an immeasurable depth; and there he beheld strange shapes of flame bending and branching and wavering like great weeds in a sea-dingle, and fiery creatures went to and fro among them. Filled with wonder he went down to the water's edge and tried it with his foot, but it was not water: it was harder than stone and slecker than glass. He stepped on it and he fell heavily, and a ringing boom ran across the lake and echoed in its shores.

At once the breeze rose to a wild Wind, roaring like a great beast, and it swept him up and flung him on the shore, and it drove him up the slopes whirling and falling like a dead leaf. He put his arms about the stem of a young birch and clung to it, and the Wind wrestled fiercely with them, trying to tear him away; but the birch was bent down to the ground by the blast and enclosed him in its branches. When at last the Wind passed on he rose and saw that the birch was naked. It was stripped of every leaf, and it wept, and tears fell from its branches like rain. He set his hand upon its white bark, saying: "Blessed be the birch! What can I do to make amends or give thanks?" He felt the answer of the tree pass up from his hand: "Nothing," it said. "Go away!

The Wind is hunting you. You do not belong here. Go away and never return!"

As he climbed back out of that dale he felt the tears of the birch trickle down his face and they were bitter on his lips. His heart was saddened as he went on his long road, and for some time he did not enter Faery again. But he could not forsake it, and when he returned his desire was still stronger to go deep into the land.

At last he found a road through the Outer Mountains, and he went on till he came to the Inner Mountains, and they were high and sheer and daunting. Yet in the end he found a pass that he could scale, and upon a day of days greatly daring he came through a narrow cleft and looked down, though he did not know it, into the Vale of Evermorn where the green surpasses the green of the meads of Outer Faery as they surpass ours in our springtime. There the air is so lucid that eyes can see the red tongues of birds as they sing on the trees upon the far side of the valley, though that is very wide and the birds are no greater than wrens.

On the inner side the mountains went down in long slopes filled with the sound of bubbling water-falls, and in great delight he hastened on. As he set foot upon the grass of the Vale he heard elven voices singing, and on a lawn beside a river bright

with lilies he came upon many maidens dancing. The speed and the grace and the ever-changing modes of their movements enchanted him, and he stepped forward towards their ring. Then suddenly they stood still, and a young maiden with flowing hair and kilted skirt came out to meet him.

She laughed as she spoke to him, saying: "You are becoming bold, Starbrow, are you not? Have you no fear what the Queen might say, if she knew of this? Unless you have her leave." He was abashed, for he became aware of his own thought and knew that she read it: that the star on his forehead was a passport to go wherever he wished; and now he knew that it was not. But she smiled as she spoke again: "Come! Now that you are here you shall dance with me"; and she took his hand and led him into the ring.

There they danced together, and for a while he knew what it was to have the swiftness and the power and the joy to accompany her. For a while. But soon as it seemed they halted again, and she stooped and took up a white flower from before her feet, and she set it in his hair. "Farewell now!" she said. "Maybe we shall meet again, by the Queen's leave."

He remembered nothing of the journey home from that meeting, until he found himself riding along the roads in his own country; and in some villages people stared at him in wonder and watched him till he rode out of sight. When he came to his own house his daughter ran out and greeted him with delight—he had returned sooner than was expected, but none too soon for those that awaited him. "Daddy!" she cried. "Where have you been? Your star is shining bright!"

When he crossed the threshold the star dimmed again; but Nell took him by the hand and led him to the hearth, and there she turned and looked at him. "Dear Man," she said, "where have you been and what have you seen? There is a flower in your hair." She lifted it gently from his head, and it lay on her hand. It seemed like a thing seen from a great distance, yet there it was, and a light came from it that cast shadows on the walls of the room, now growing dark in the evening. The shadow of the man before her loomed up and its great head was bowed over her. "You look like a giant, Dad," said his son, who had not spoken before.

The flower did not wither nor grow dim; and they kept it as a secret and a treasure. The smith made a little casket with a key for it, and there it lay and was handed down for many generations in his kin; and those who inherited the key would at times open the casket and look long at the Living Flower, till the casket closed again: the time of its shutting was not theirs to choose.

The years did not halt in the village. Many now had passed. At the Children's Feast when he received the star the smith was not yet ten years old. Then came another Twenty-four Feast, by which time Alf had become Master Cook and had chosen a new apprentice, Harper. Twelve years later the smith had returned with the Living Flower; and now another Children's Twenty-four Feast was due in the winter to come. One day in that year Smith was walking in the woods of Outer Faery, and it was autumn. Golden leaves were on the boughs and red leaves were on the ground. Footsteps came behind him, but he did not heed them or turn round, for he was deep in thought.

On that visit he had received a summons and had made a far journey. Longer it seemed to him than any he had yet made. He was guided and guarded, but he had little memory of the ways that he had taken; for often he had been blindfolded by mist or by shadow, until at last he came to a high place under a night-sky of innumerable stars. There he was brought before the Queen herself. She wore no crown and had no throne. She stood there in her majesty and her glory, and all about her was a great host shimmering and glittering like the stars above; but she was taller than the points of their great spears, and upon her head there burned a white flame. She made a sign for him to approach, and trembling he stepped forward. A high clear trumpet sounded, and behold! they were alone.

He stood before her, and he did not kneel in courtesy, for he was dismayed and felt that for one so lowly all gestures were in vain. At length he looked up and beheld her face and her eyes bent gravely upon him; and he was troubled and amazed, for in that moment he knew her again: the fair maid of the Green Vale, the dancer at whose feet the flowers sprang. She smiled seeing his memory, and drew towards him; and they spoke long together, for the most part without words, and he learned many things in her thought, some of which gave him joy, and others filled him with grief. Then his mind turned back retracing his life, until he came to the day of the Children's Feast and the coming of the star, and suddenly he saw again the little dancing figure with its wand, and in shame he lowered his eyes from the Queen's beauty.

But she laughed again as she had laughed in the Vale of Evermorn. "Do not be grieved for me, Starbrow," she said. "Nor too much ashamed of you own folk. Better a little doll, maybe, than no memory of Faery at all. For some the only glimpse. For some the awaking. Ever since that day you have desired in your heart to see me, and I have granted your wish. But I can give you no more. Now at farewell I will make you my messenger. If you meet the King, say to him: *The time has come. Let him choose.*"

"But Lady of Faery," he stammered, "where then is the King?" For he had asked this question many times of the people of Faery, and they had all said the same: "He has not told us."

And the Queen answered: "If he has not told you, Starbrow, then I may not. But he makes many journeys and may be met in unlikely places. Now kneel of your courtesy."

Then he knelt, and she stooped and laid her hand on his head, and a great stillness came upon him; and he seemed to be both in the World and in Faery, and also outside them and surveying them, so that he was at once in bereavement, and in ownership, and in peace. When after a while the stillness passed he raised his head and stood up. The dawn was in the sky and the stars were pale, and the Queen was gone. Far off he heard the echo of a trumpet in the mountains. The high field where he stood was silent and empty; and he knew that his way now led back to bereavement.

That meeting-place was now far behind him, and here he was, walking among the fallen leaves, pondering all that he had seen and learned. The footsteps came nearer. Then suddenly a voice said at his side: "Are you going my way, Starbrow?"

He started and came out of his thoughts, and he saw a man beside him. He was tall, and he walked lightly and quickly; he was dressed all in dark green and wore a hood that partly overshadowed his face. The smith was puzzled, for only the people of Faery called him "Starbrow," but he could not remember ever having seen this man there before; and yet he felt uneasily that he should know him. "What way are you going then?" he said.

"I am going back to your village now," the man answered, "and I hope that you are also returning."

"I am indeed," said the smith. "Let us walk together. But now something has come back to my mind. Before I began my homeward journey a Great Lady gave me a message, but we shall soon be passing from Faery, and I do not think that I shall ever return. Will you?"

"Yes, I shall. You may give the message to me."

"But the message was to the King. Do you know where to find him?"

"I do. What was the message?"

"The Lady only asked me to say to him: *The time has come. Let him choose.*"

"I understand. Trouble yourself no further."

They went on then side by side in silence save for the rustle of the leaves about their feet; but after a few miles while they were still within the bounds of Faery the man halted. He turned towards the smith and threw back his hood. Then the smith knew him. He was Alf the Prentice, as the smith still called him in his own mind, remembering always the day when as a youth Alf had stood in the Hall, holding the bright knife for the cutting of the Cake, and his eyes had gleamed in the light of the candles. He must be an old man now, for he had been Master Cook for many years; but here standing under the eaves of the Outer Wood he looked like the apprentice of long ago, though more masterly: there was no grey in his hair nor line on his face, and his eyes gleamed as if they reflected a light.

"I should like to speak to you, Smith Smithson, before we go back to your country," he said. The smith wondered at that, for he himself had often wished to talk to Alf, but had never been able to do so. Alf had always greeted him kindly and had looked at him with friendly eyes, but had seemed to avoid talking to him alone. He was looking now at the smith with friendly eyes; but he lifted his hand and with his forefinger touched the star on his brow. The gleam left his eyes, and then the smith knew that it had come from the star, and that it must have been shining brightly but now was dimmed. He was surprised and drew away angrily.

"Do you not think, Master Smith," said Alf, "that it is time for you to give this thing up?"

"What is that to you, Master Cook?" he answered. "And why should I do so? Isn't it mine? It came to me, and may a man not keep things that come to him so, at the least as a remembrance?"

"Some things. Those that are free gifts and given for remembrance. But others are not so given. They cannot belong to a man for ever, nor be treasured as heirlooms. They are lent. You have not thought, perhaps, that someone else may need this thing. But it is so. Time is pressing."

Then the smith was troubled, for he was a generous man, and he remembered with gratitude all that the star had brought to him. "Then what should I do?" he asked. "Should I give it to one of the Great in Faery? Should I give it to the King?" And as he said this a hope sprang in his heart that on such an errand he might once more enter Faery.

"You could give it to me," said Alf, "but you might find that too hard. Will you come with me to my store-room and put it back in the box where your grandfather laid it?"

"I did not know that," said the smith.

"No one knew but me. I was the only one with him."

"Then I suppose that you know how he came by the star, and why he put it in the box?"

"He brought it from Faery: that you know without asking," Alf answered. "He left it behind in the hope that it might come to you, his only grandchild. So he told me, for he thought that I could arrange that. He was your mother's father. I do not know whether she told you much about him, if indeed she knew much to tell. Rider was his name, and he was a great traveller: he had seen many things and could do many things before he settled down and became Master Cook. But he went away when you were only two years old— and they could find no one better to follow him than Nokes, poor man. Still, as we expected, I became Master in time. This year I shall make another Great Cake: the only Cook, as far as is remembered, ever to make a second one. I wish to put the star in it."

"Very well, you shall have it," said the smith. He looked at Alf as if he was trying to read his thought. "Do you know who will find it?"

"What is that to you, Master Smith?"

"I should like to know, if you do, Master Cook. It might make it easier for me to part with a thing so dear to me. My daughter's child is too young."

"It might and it might not. We shall see," said Alf.

They said no more, and they went on their way until they passed out of Faery and came back at last to the village. Then they walked to the Hall; and in the world the sun was now setting and a red light was in the windows. The gilded carvings on the great door glowed, and strange faces of many colours looked down from the water-spouts under the roof. Not long ago the Hall had been re-glazed and re-painted, and there had been much debate on the Council about it. Some disliked it and called it "new-fangled," but some with more knowledge knew that it was a return to old custom. Still, since it had cost no one a penny and the Master Cook must have paid for it himself, he was allowed to have his own way. But the smith had not seen it in such a light before, and he stood and looked at the Hall in wonder, forgetting his errand.

He felt a touch on his arm, and Alf led him round to a small door at the back. He opened it and led the smith down a dark passage into the store-room. There he lit a tall candle, and unlocking a cupboard he took down from a shelf the black box. It was polished now and adorned with silver scrolls.

He raised the lid and showed it to the smith.

One small compartment was empty; the others were now filled with spices, fresh and pungent, and the smith's eyes began to water. He put his hand to his forehead, and the star came away readily; but he felt a sudden stab of pain, and tears ran down his face. Though the star shone brightly again as it lay in his hand, he could not see it, except as a blurred dazzle of light that seemed far away.

"I cannot see clearly," he said. "You must put it in for me." He held out his hand, and Alf took the star and laid it in its place, and it went dark.

The smith turned away without another word and groped his way to the door. On the threshold he found that his sight had cleared again. It was evening and the Even-star was shining in a luminous sky close to the Moon. As he stood for a moment looking at their beauty, he felt a hand on his shoulder and turned.

"You gave me the star freely," said Alf. "If you still wish to know to which child it will go, I will tell you."

"I do indeed."

"It shall go to any one that you appoint."

The smith was taken aback and did not answer at once. "Well," he said hesitating, "I wonder what you may think of my choice. I believe you have little reason to love the name of Nokes, but, well, his little great-grandson, Nokes of Townsend's Tim, is coming to the Feast. Nokes of Townsend is quite different."

"I have observed that," said Alf. "He had a wise mother."

"Yes, my Nell's sister. But apart from the kinship I love little Tim. Though he's not an obvious choice."

Alf smiled. "Neither were you," he said. "But I agree. Indeed I had already chosen Tim."

"Then why did you ask me to choose?"

"The Queen wished me to do so. If you had chosen differently I should have given way."

The smith looked long at Alf. Then suddenly he bowed low. "I understand at last, sir," he said. "You have done us too much honour."

"I have been repaid," said Alf. "Go home now in peace!"

When the smith reached his own house on the western outskirts of the village he found his son by the door of the forge. He had just locked it, for the day's work was done, and now he stood looking up the white road by which his father used to return from his journeys. Hearing footsteps he turned in surprise to see him coming from the village, and he ran forward to meet him. He put his arms about him in loving welcome.

"I've been hoping for you since yesterday, Dad," he said. Then looking into his father's face he said anxiously: "How tired you look! You have walked far, maybe?"

"Very far indeed, my son. All the way from Daybreak to Evening."

They went into the house together, and it was dark except for the fire flickering on the hearth. His son lit candles, and for a while they sat by the fire without speaking; for a great weariness and bereavement was on the smith. At last he looked round, as if coming to himself, and he said: "Why are we alone?"

His son looked hard at him. "Why? Mother's over at Minor, at Nan's. It's the little lad's second birthday. They hoped you would be there too."

"Ah yes. I ought to have been. I should have been, Ned, but I was delayed; and I have had matters to think of that put all else out of mind for a time. But I did not forget Tomling."

He put his hand in his breast and drew out a little wallet of soft leather. "I have brought him something. A trinket old Nokes maybe would call it—but it comes out of Faery, Ned." Out of the wallet he took a little thing of silver. It was like the smooth stem of a tiny lily from the top of which came three delicate flowers, bending down like shapely bells. And bells they were, for when he shook them gently each flower rang with a small clear note. At the sweet sound the candles flickered and then for a moment shone with a white light.

Ned's eyes were wide with wonder. "May I look at it, Dad?" he said. He took it with careful fingers and peered into the flowers. "The work is a marvel!" he said. "And, Dad, there is a scent in the bells: a scent that reminds me of, reminds me, well, of something I've forgotten."

"Yes, the scent comes for a little while after the bells have rung. But don't fear to handle it, Ned. It was made for a babe to play with. He can do it no harm, and he'll take none from it."

The smith put the gift back in the wallet and stowed it away. "I'll take it over to Wootton Minor myself tomorrow," he said. "Nan and her Tom, and Mother, will forgive me, maybe. As for Tomling, his time has not come yet for the counting of days . . . and of weeks, and of months, and of years."

"That's right. You go, Dad. I'd be glad to go with you; but it will be some time before I can get over to Minor. I couldn't have gone today, even if I hadn't waited here for you. There's a lot of work in hand, and more coming in."

"No, no, Smith's son! Make it a holiday! The name of grandfather hasn't weakened my arms yet a while. Let the work come! There'll be two pairs of hands to tackle it now, all working days. I shall not be going on journeys again, Ned: not on long ones, if you understand me."

"It's that way is it, Dad? I wondered what had become of the star. That's hard." He took his father's hand. "I'm grieved for you; but there's good in it too, for this house. Do you know, Master Smith, there is much you can teach me yet, if you have the time. And I do not mean only the working of iron."

They had supper together, and long after they had finished they still sat at the table, while the smith told his son of his last journey in Faery, and of other things that came to his mind—but about the choice of the next holder of the star he said nothing.

At last his son looked at him, and "Father," he said, "do you remember the day when you came back with the Flower? And I said that you looked like a giant by your shadow. The shadow was the truth. So it was the Queen herself that you danced with! Yet you have given up the star. I hope it may go to someone as worthy. The child should be grateful."

"The child won't know," said the smith. "That's the way with such gifts. Well, there it is. I have handed it on and come back to hammer and tongs."

It is a strange thing, but old Nokes, who had scoffed at his apprentice, had never been able to put out of his mind the disappearance of the star in the Cake, although that event had happened so many years ago. He had grown fat and lazy, and retired from his office when he was sixty (no great age in the village). He was now near the end of his eighties, and was of enormous bulk, for he still ate heavily and doted on sugar. Most of his days, when not at table, he spent in a big chair by the window of his cottage, or by the door if it was fine weather. He liked talking, since he still had many opinions to air; but lately his talk mostly turned to the one Great Cake that he had made (as he was now firmly convinced), for whenever he fell asleep it came into his dreams. Prentice sometimes stopped for a word or two. So the old cook still called him, and he expected himself to be called Master. That Prentice was careful to do; which was a point in his favour, though there were others that Nokes was more fond of.

One afternoon Nokes was nodding in his chair by the door after his dinner. He woke with a start to find Prentice standing by and looking down at him. "Hullo!" he said. "I'm glad to see you, for that cake's been on my mind again. I was thinking of it just now in fact. It was the best cake I ever made, and that's saying something. But perhaps you have forgotten it."

"No, Master. I remember it very well. But what

is troubling you? It was a good cake, and it was enjoyed and praised."

"Of course. I made it. But that doesn't trouble me. It's the little trinket, the star. I cannot make up my mind what became of it. Of course it wouldn't melt. I only said that to stop the children from being frightened. I have wondered if one of them did not swallow it. But is that likely? You might swallow one of those little coins and not notice it, but not that star. It was small but it had sharp points."

"Yes, Master. But do you really know what the star was made of? Don't trouble your mind about it. Someone swallowed it, I assure you."

"Then who? Well, I've a long memory, and that day sticks in it somehow. I can recall all the children's names. Let me think. It must have been Miller's Molly! She was greedy and bolted her food. She's as fat as a sack now."

"Yes, there are some folk who get like that, Master. But Molly did not bolt her cake. She found two trinkets in her slice."

"Oh, did she? Well, it was Cooper's Harry then. A barrel of a boy with a big mouth like a frog's."

"I should have said, Master, that he was a nice boy with a large friendly grin. Anyway he was so careful that he took his slice to pieces before he ate it. He found nothing but cake."

"Then it must have been that little pale girl,

Draper's Lily. She used to swallow pins as a baby and came to no harm."

"Not Lily, Master. She only ate the paste and the sugar, and gave the inside to the boy that sat next to her."

"Then I give up. Who was it? You seem to have been watching very closely. If you're not making it all up."

"It was the Smith's son, Master; and I think it was good for him."

"Go on!" laughed old Nokes. "I ought to have known you were having a game with me. Don't be ridiculous! Smith was a quiet slow boy then. He makes more noise now: a bit of a songster, I hear; but he's cautious. No risks for him. Chews twice before he swallows, and always did, if you take my meaning."

"I do, Master. Well, if you won't believe it was Smith, I can't help you. Perhaps it doesn't matter much now. Will it ease your mind if I tell you that the star is back in the box now? Here it is!"

Prentice was wearing a dark green cloak, which Nokes now noticed for the first time. From its folds he produced the black box and opened it under the old cook's nose. "There is the star, Master, down in the corner."

Old Nokes began coughing and sneezing, but at last he looked into the box. "So it is!" he said. "At least it looks like it."

"It is the same one, Master. I put it there myself a few days ago. It will go back in the Great Cake this winter."

"A-ha!" said Nokes, leering at Prentice; and then he laughed till he shook like a jelly. "I see, I see! Twenty-four children and twenty-four lucky bits, and the star was one extra. So you nipped it out before the baking and kept it for another time. You were always a tricky fellow: nimble one might say. And thrifty: wouldn't waste a bee's knee of butter. Ha, ha, ha! So that was the way of it. I might have guessed. Well, that's cleared up. Now I can have a nap in peace." He settled down in his chair. "Mind that prentice-man of yours plays you no tricks! The artful don't know all the arts, they say." He closed his eyes.

"Goodbye, Master!" said Prentice, shutting the box with such a snap that the cook opened his eyes again. "Nokes," he said, "your knowledge is so great that I have only twice ventured to tell you anything. I told you that the star came from Faery; and I have told you that it went to the smith. You laughed at me. Now at parting I will tell you one thing more. Don't laugh again! You are a vain old fraud, fat, idle and sly. I did most of your work. Without thanks you learned all that you could from me—except respect for Faery, and a little courtesy. You have not even enough to bid me good day."

"If it comes to courtesy," said Nokes, "I see none in calling your elders and betters by ill names. Take your Fairy and your nonsense somewhere else! Good day to you, if that's what you're waiting for. Now go along with you!" He flapped his hand mockingly. "If you've got one of your fairy friends hidden in the Kitchen, send him to me and I'll have a look at him. If he waves his little wand and makes me thin again, I'll think better of him," he laughed.

"Would you spare a few moments for the King of Faery?" the other answered. To Nokes's dismay he grew taller as he spoke. He threw back his cloak. He was dressed like a Master Cook at a Feast, but his white garments shimmered and glinted, and on his forehead was a great jewel like a radiant star. His face was young but stern.

"Old man," he said, "you are at least not my elder. As to my better: you have often sneered at me behind my back. Do you challenge me now openly?" He stepped forward, and Nokes shrank from him, trembling. He tried to shout for help but found that he could hardly whisper.

"No, sir!" he croaked. "Don't do me a harm! I'm only a poor old man."

The King's face softened. "Alas, yes! You speak the truth. Do not be afraid! Be at ease! But will you not expect the King of Faery to do something for you before he leaves you? I grant you your wish. Farewell! Now go to sleep!"

He wrapped his cloak about him again and went away towards the Hall; but before he was out of sight the old cook's goggling eyes had shut and he was snoring.

When the old cook woke again the sun was going down. He rubbed his eyes and shivered a little, for the autumn air was chilly. "Ugh! What a dream!" he said. "It must have been that pork at dinner."

From that day he became so afraid of having more bad dreams of that sort that he hardly dared eat anything for fear that it might upset him, and his meals became very short and plain. He soon became lean, and his clothes and his skin hung on him in folds and creases. The children called him old Rag-and-Bones. Then for a time he found that he could get about the village again and walk with no more help than a stick; and he lived many years longer than he would otherwise have done. Indeed it is said that he just made his century: the only memorable thing he ever achieved. But till his last year he could be heard saying to any that would listen to his tale: "Alarming, you might call it; but a silly dream, when you come to think of it. King o' Fairy! Why, he hadn't no wand. And if you stop eating you grow thinner. That's nat-

ural. Stands to reason. There ain't no magic in
it."

The time for the Twenty-four Feast came round.
Smith was there to sing songs and his wife to
help with the children. Smith looked at them as
they sang and danced, and he thought that they
were more beautiful and lively than they had been
in his boyhood—for a moment it crossed his mind
to wonder what Alf might have been doing in his
spare time. Any one of them seemed fit to find the
star. But his eyes were mostly on Tim: a rather
plump little boy, clumsy in the dances, but with
a sweet voice in the singing. At table he sat silent,
watching the sharpening of the knife and the cutting of the Cake. Suddenly, he piped up:
"Dear Mr. Cook, only cut me a small slice
please. I've eaten so much already, I feel rather
full."

"All right, Tim," said Alf. "I'll cut you a special
slice. I think you'll find it go down easily."

Smith watched as Tim ate his cake slowly, but
wtih evident pleasure; though when he found no
trinket or coin in it he looked disappointed. But
soon a light began to shine in his eyes, and he
laughed and became merry, and sang softly to himself. Then he got up and began to dance all alone
with an odd grace that he had never shown before.
The children all laughed and clapped.

"All is well then," thought Smith. "So you are my heir. I wonder what strange places the star will lead you to? Poor old Nokes. Still I suppose he will never know what a shocking thing has happened in his family."

He never did. But one thing happened at that Feast that pleased him mightily. Before it was over the Master Cook took leave of the children and of all the others that were present.

"I will say goodbye now," he said. "In a day or two I shall be going away. Master Harper is quite ready to take over. He is a very good cook, and as you know he comes from your own village. I shall go back home. I do not think you will miss me."

The children said goodbye cheerfully, and thanked the Cook prettily for his beautiful Cake. Only little Tim took his hand and said quietly, "I'm sorry."

In the village there were in fact several families that did miss Alf for some time. A few of his friends, especially Smith and Harper, grieved at his going, and they kept the Hall gilded and painted in memory of Alf. Most people, however, were content. They had had him for a very long time and were not sorry to have a change. But old Nokes thumped his stick on the floor and said roundly: "He's gone at last! And I'm glad for one

I never liked him. He was artful. Too nimble, you might say."

Farmer Giles
of Ham

Aegidii Ahenobarbi Julii Agricole de Hammo
Domini de Domito
Aule Draconarie Comitis
Regni Minimi Regis et Basilei
mira facinora et mirabilis
exortus

or in the vulgar tongue

The Rise and Wonderful Adventures of
Farmer Giles, Lord of Tame,
Count of Worminghall
and King of
the Little Kingdom

To C. H. Wilkinson

Foreword

OF THE HISTORY of the Little Kingdom few fragments have survived; but by chance an account of its origin has been preserved: a legend, perhaps, rather than an account; for it is evidently a late compilation, full of marvels, derived not from sober annals, but from the popular lays to which its author frequently refers. For him the events that he records lay already in a distant past; but he seems, nonetheless, to have lived himself in the lands of the Little Kingdom. Such geographical knowledge as he shows (it is not his strong point) is of that country, while of regions outside it, north or west, he is plainly ignorant.

An excuse for presenting a translation of this curious tale, out of its very insular Latin into the modern tongue of the United Kingdom, may be found in the glimpse that it affords of life in a dark period of the history of Britain, not to mention the light that it throws on the origin of some difficult place-names. Some may find the character and adventures of its hero attractive in themselves.

The boundaries of the Little Kingdom, either in time or space, are not easy to determine from the scanty evidence. Since Brutus came to Britain many kings and realms have come and gone. The partition under Locrin, Camber, and Albanac, was only the first of many shifting divisions. What with the love of petty independence on the one hand, and on the other the greed of kings for wider realms, the years were filled with swift alternations of war and peace, of mirth and woe, as historians of the reign of Arthur tell us: a time of unsettled frontiers, when men might rise or fall suddenly, and songwriters had abundant material and eager audiences. Somewhere in those long years, after the days of King Coel maybe, but before Arthur or the Seven Kingdoms of the English, we must place the events here related; and their scene is the valley of the Thames, with an excursion north-west to the walls of Wales.

The capital of the Little Kingdom was evidently, as is ours, in its south-east corner, but its confines are vague. It seems never to have reached far up the Thames into the West, nor beyond Otmoor to the North; its eastern borders are dubious. There are indications in a fragmentary legend of Georgius son of Giles and his page Suovetaurilius

(Suet) that at one time an outpost against the Middle Kingdom was maintained at Farthingho. But that situation does not concern this story, which is now presented without alteration or further comment, though the original grandiose title has been suitably reduced to *Farmer Giles of Ham.*

ÆGIDIUS DE HAMMO was a man who lived in the midmost parts of the Island of Britain. In full his name was Ægidius Ahenobarbus Julius Agricola de Hammo; for people were richly endowed with names in those days, now long ago, when this island was still happily divided into many kingdoms. There was more time then, and folk were fewer, so that most men were distinguished. However, those days are now over, so I will in what follows give the man his name shortly, and in the vulgar form: he was Farmer Giles of Ham, and he had a red beard. Ham was only a village, but villages were proud and independent still in those days.

Farmer Giles had a dog. The dog's name was Garm. Dogs had to be content with short names in the vernacular: the Book-latin was reserved for their betters. Garm could not talk even dog-latin; but he could use the vulgar tongue (as could most dogs of his day) either to bully or to brag or to wheedle in. Bullying was for beggars and trespassers, bragging for other dogs, and wheedling for his master. Garm was both proud and afraid of Giles, who could bully and brag better than he could.

The time was not one of hurry or bustle. But bustle has very little to do with business. Men did their work without it; and they got through a deal both of work and of talk. There was plenty to talk about, for memorable events occurred very frequently. But at the moment when this tale begins nothing memorable had, in fact, happened in Ham for quite a long time. Which suited Farmer Giles down to the ground: he was a slow sort of fellow, rather set in his ways, and taken up with his own affairs. He had his hands full (he said) keeping the wolf from the door: that is, keeping himself as fat and comfortable as his father before him. The dog was busy helping him. Neither of them gave much thought to the Wide World outside their fields, the village, and the nearest market.

But the Wide World was there. The forest was not far off, and away west and north were the Wild Hills, and the dubious marches of the mountain-country. And among other things still at large there were giants: rude and uncultured folk, and troublesome at times. There was one giant in particular, larger and more stupid than his fellows. I find no mention of his name in the histories, but it does not matter. He was very large, his walking-stick was like a tree, and his tread was heavy. He brushed elms aside like tall grasses; and he was the ruin of roads and the desolation of gardens, for his great feet made holes in them as deep as wells; if he stumbled into a house, that was the end of it. And all this damage he did wherever he went, for his head was far above the roofs of houses and left his feet to look after themselves. He was near-sighted and also rather deaf. Fortunately he lived far off in the Wild, and seldom visited the lands inhabited by men, at least not on purpose. He had a great tumbledown house away up in the mountains; but he had very few friends, owing to his deafness and his stupidity, and the scarcity of giants. He used to go out walking in the Wild Hills and in the empty regions at the feet of the mountains, all by himself.

One fine summer's day this giant went out for a walk, and wandered aimlessly along, doing a great deal of damage in the woods. Suddenly he noticed that the sun was setting, and felt that his suppertime was drawing near; but he discovered that he was in a part of the country that he did not know at all and had lost his way. Making a wrong guess at the right direction he walked and he walked until it was dark night. Then he sat down and waited for the moon to rise. Then he walked and walked in the moonlight, striding out with a will, for he was anxious to get home. He had left his best copper pot on the fire, and feared that the bottom would be burned. But his back was to the mountains, and he was already in the lands inhabited by men. He was, indeed, now drawing near to the farm of Ægidius Ahenobarbus Julius Agricola and the village called (in the vulgar tongue) Ham.

It was a fine night. The cows were in the fields, and Farmer Giles's dog had got out and gone for a walk on his own account. He had a fancy for moonshine, and rabbits. He had no idea, of course, that a giant was also out for a walk. That would have given him a good reason for going out without leave, but a still better reason for staying quiet in the kitchen. At about two o'clock the giant arrived in Farmer Giles's fields, broke the hedges, trampled on the crops, and flattened the mowing-grass. In five minutes he had done more damage than the royal fox-hunt could have done in five days.

Garm heard a thump-thump coming along the riverbank, and he ran to the west side of the low hill on which the farmhouse stood, just to see what was happening. Suddenly he saw the giant stride right across the river and tread upon Gala-

thea, the farmer's favourite cow, squashing the poor beast as flat as the farmer could have squashed a blackbeetle.

That was more than enough for Garm. He gave a yelp of fright and bolted home. Quite forgetting

that he was out without leave, he came and barked and yammered underneath his master's bedroom window. There was no answer for a long time. Farmer Giles was not easily wakened. "Help! help! help!" cried Garm. The window opened suddenly and a well-aimed bottle came flying out.

"Ow!" said the dog, jumping aside with practised skill. "Help! help! help!"

Out popped the farmer's head. "Drat you, dog! What be you a-doing?" said he.

"Nothing," said the dog.

"I'll give you nothing! I'll flay the skin off you in the morning," said the farmer, slamming the window.

"Help! help! help!" cried the dog.

Out came Giles's head again. "I'll kill you, if you make another sound," he said. "What's come to you, you fool?"

"Nothing," said the dog; "but something's come to you."

"What d'you mean?" said Giles, startled in the midst of his rage. Never before had Garm answered him saucily.

"There's a giant in your fields, an enormous giant; and he's coming this way," said the dog. "Help! help! He is trampling on your sheep. He has stamped on poor Galathea, and she's as flat as a doormat. Help! help! He's bursting all your hedges, and he's crushing all your crops. You must be bold and quick, master, or you will soon have nothing left. Help!" Garm began to howl.

"Shut up!" said the farmer, and he shut the window. "Lord-a-mercy!" he said to himself; and though the night was warm, he shivered and shook.

"Get back to bed and don't be a fool!" said his wife. "And drown that dog in the morning. There is no call to believe what a dog says: they'll tell any tale, when caught truant or thieving."

"May be, Agatha," said he, "and may be not. But there's something going on in my fields, or Garm's a rabbit. That dog was frightened. And why should he come yammering in the night when he could sneak in at the back door with the milk in the morning?"

"Don't stand there arguing!" said she. "If you believe the dog, then take his advice: be bold and quick!"

"Easier said than done," answered Giles; for, indeed, he believed quite half of Garm's tale. In the small hours of the night giants seem less un-likely.

Still, property is property; and Farmer Giles had a short way with trespassers that few could out-face. So he pulled on his breeches, and went down into the kitchen and took his blunderbuss from the wall. Some may well ask what a blunderbuss was. Indeed, this very question, it is said, was put to the Four Wise Clerks of Oxenford, and after thought they replied: "A blunderbuss is a short gun with a large bore firing many balls or slugs, and capable of doing execution within a limited range without exact aim. (Now superseded in civilized countries by other firearms.)"

However, Farmer Giles's blunderbuss had a wide mouth that opened like a horn, and it did not fire balls or slugs, but anything that he could spare to stuff in. And it did not do execution, because he seldom loaded it, and never let it off. The sight of it was usually enough for his purpose. And this country was not yet civilized, for the blunderbuss was not superseded: it was indeed the only kind of gun that there was, and rare at that. People preferred bows and arrows and used gunpowder mostly for fireworks.

Well then, Farmer Giles took down the blunderbuss, and he put in a good charge of powder, just in case extreme measures should be required; and into the wide mouth he stuffed old nails and bits of wire, pieces of broken pot, bones and stones and other rubbish. Then he drew on his top-boots and his overcoat, and he went out through the kitchen garden.

The moon was low behind him, and he could see nothing worse than the long black shadows of bushes and trees; but he could hear a dreadful stamping-stumping coming up the side of the hill. He did not feel either bold or quick, whatever Agatha might say; but he was more anxious about his property than his skin. So, feeling a bit loose about the belt, he walked towards the brow of the hill.

Suddenly up over the edge of it the giant's face appeared, pale in the moonlight, which glittered in his large round eyes. His feet were still far below, making holes in the fields. The moon dazzled the giant and he did not see the farmer; but Farmer

Giles saw him and was scared out of his wits. He pulled the trigger without thinking, and the blunderbuss went off with a staggering bang. By luck it was pointed more or less at the giant's large ugly face. Out flew the rubbish, and the stones and the bones, and the bits of crock and wire, and half a dozen nails. And since the range was indeed limited, by chance and no choice of the farmer's many of these things struck the giant: a piece of pot went in his eye, and a large nail stuck in his nose.

"Blast!" said the giant in his vulgar fashion. "I'm stung!" The noise had made no impression on him (he was rather deaf), but he did not like the nail. It was a long time since he had met any insect fierce enough to pierce his thick skin; but he had heard tell that away East, in the Fens, there were dragon-flies that could bite like hot pincers. He thought that he must have run into something of the kind.

"Nasty unhealthy parts, evidently," said he. "I shan't go any further this way tonight."

So he picked up a couple of sheep off the hillside, to eat when he got home, and went back over the river, making off about nor-nor-west at a great pace. He found his way home again in the end, for he was at last going in the right direction; but the bottom was burned off his copper pot.

As for Farmer Giles, when the blunderbuss went off it knocked him over flat on his back; and there he lay looking at the sky and wondering if the giant's feet would miss him as they passed by. But nothing happened, and the stamping-stumping died away in the distance. So he got up, rubbed his shoulder, and picked up the blunderbuss. Then suddenly he heard the sound of people cheering.

Most of the people of Ham had been looking out of their windows; a few had put on their clothes and come out (after the giant had gone away). Some were now running up the hill shouting.

The villagers had heard the horrible thump-thump of the giant's feet, and most of them had immediately got under the bed-clothes; some had got under the beds. But Garm was both proud and frightened of his master. He thought him terrible and splendid, when he was angry; and he naturally thought that any giant would think the same. So, as soon as he saw Giles come out with the blunderbuss (a sign of great wrath as a rule), he rushed off to the village, barking and crying:

"Come out! Come out! Come out! Get up! Get up! Come and see my great master! He is bold and quick. He is going to shoot a giant for trespassing. Come out!"

The top of the hill could be seen from most of the houses. When the people and the dog saw the giant's face rise above it, they quailed and held their breath, and all but the dog among them thought that this would prove a matter too big for Giles to deal with. Then the blunderbuss went bang, and the giant turned suddenly and went away, and in their amazement and their joy they clapped and cheered, and Garm nearly barked his head off.

"Hooray!" they shouted. "That will learn him! Master Ægidius has given him what for. Now he will go home and die, and serve him right and proper." Then they all cheered again together. But even as they cheered, they took note for their own profit that after all this blunderbuss could really be fired. There had been some debate in the village inns on that point; but now the matter was settled. Farmer Giles had little trouble with trespassers after that.

When all seemed safe some of the bolder folk came right up the hill and shook hands with Farmer Giles. A few—the parson, and the blacksmith, and the miller, and one or two other persons of importance—slapped him on the back. That did not please him (his shoulder was very sore), but he felt obliged to invite them into his house. They sat round in the kitchen drinking his health and loudly praising him. He made no effort to hide his yawns, but as long as the drink lasted they took no notice. By the time they had

all had one or two (and the farmer two or three), he began to feel quite bold; when they had all had two or three (and he himself five or six), he felt as bold as his dog thought him. They parted good friends; and he slapped their backs heartily. His hands were large, red, and thick; so he had his revenge.

Next day he found that the news had grown in

the telling, and he had become an important local figure. By the middle of the next week the news had spread to all the villages within twenty miles. He had become the Hero of the Countryside. Very pleasant he found it. Next market day he got enough free drink to float a boat: that is to say, he nearly had his fill, and came home singing old heroic songs.

At last even the King got to hear it. The capital of that realm, the Middle Kingdom of the island in those happy days, was some twenty leagues distant from Ham, and they paid little heed at court, as a

rule, to the doings of rustics in the provinces. But so prompt an expulsion of a giant so injurious seemed worthy of note and of some little courtesy. So in due course—that is, in about three months, and on the feast of St. Michael—the King sent a magnificent letter. It was written in red upon white parchment, and expressed the royal approbation of "our loyal subject and well-beloved Ægidius Ahenobarbus Julius Agricola de Hammo."

The letter was signed with a red blot; but the court scribe had added: **Ego Augustus Bonifacius Ambrosius Aurelianus Antoninus Pius et Magnificus, dux, rex, tyrannus, et basileus Mediterranearum Partium, subscribo;** and a large red seal was attached. So the document was plainly genuine. It afforded great pleasure to Giles, and was much admired, especially when it was discovered that one could get a seat and a drink by the farmer's fire by asking to look at it.

Better than the testimonial was the accompanying gift. The King sent a belt and a long sword. To tell the truth the King had never used the sword himself. It belonged to the family and had been hanging in his armoury time out of mind. The armourer could not say how it came there, or what might be the use of it. Plain heavy swords of that kind were out of fashion at court just then, so the King thought it the very thing for a present to a rustic. But Farmer Giles was delighted, and his local reputation became enormous.

Giles much enjoyed the turn of events. So did

his dog. He never got his promised whipping. Giles was a just man according to his lights; in his heart he gave a fair share of the credit to Garm, though he never went so far as to mention it. He continued to throw hard words and hard things at

the dog when he felt inclined, but he winked at many little outings. Garm took to walking far afield. The farmer went about with a high step, and luck smiled on him. The autumn and early winter work went well. All seemed set fair—until the dragon came.

In those days dragons were already getting scarce in the island. None had been seen in the midland realm of Augustus Bonifacius for many a year. There were, of course, the dubious marches and the uninhabited mountains, westward and northward, but they were a long way off. In those parts once upon a time there had dwelt a number of dragons of one kind and another, and they had made raids far and wide. But the Middle Kingdom was in those days famous for the daring of the King's knights, and so many stray dragons had been killed, or had returned with grave damage, that the others gave up going that way.

It was still the custom for Dragon's Tail to be served up at the King's Christmas Feast; and each year a knight was chosen for the duty of hunting. He was supposed to set out upon St. Nicholas' Day and come home with a dragon's tail not later than the eve of the feast. But for many years now the Royal Cook had made a marvellous confection, a Mock Dragon's Tail of cake and almond-paste, with cunning scales of hard icing-sugar. The chosen knight then carried this into the hall on Christmas Eve, while the fiddles played and the trumpets rang. The Mock Dragon's Tail was eaten after dinner on Christmas Day, and everybody said (to please the cook) that it tasted much better than Real Tail.

That was the situation when a real dragon turned up again. The giant was largely to blame. After his adventure he used to go about in the mountains visiting his scattered relations more than had been his custom, and much more than they liked. For he was always trying to borrow a large copper pot. But whether he got the loan of one or not, he would sit and talk in his long-winded lumbering fashion about the excellent country down away East, and all the wonders of the Wide World. He had got it into his head that he was a great and daring traveller.

"A nice land," he would say, "pretty flat, soft to the feet, and plenty to eat for the taking: cows, you know, and sheep all over the place, easy to spot, if you look carefully."

"But what about the people?" said they.

"I never saw any," said he. "There was not a knight to be seen or heard, my dear fellows. Nothing worse than a few stinging flies by the river."

"Why don't you go back and stay there?" said they.

"Oh well, there's no place like home, they say," said he. "But maybe I shall go back one day when I have a mind. And anyway I went there once, which is more than most folk can say. Now about that copper pot."

"And these rich lands," they would hurriedly ask, "these delectable regions full of undefended cattle, which way do they lie? And how far off?"

"Oh," he would answer, "away east or sou'east. But it's a long journey." And then he would give such an exaggerated account of the distance that he had walked, and the woods, hills, and plains that he had crossed, that none of the other less long-legged giants ever set out. Still, the talk got about.

Then the warm summer was followed by a hard winter. It was bitter cold in the mountains and food was scarce. The talk got louder. Lowland sheep and kine from the deep pastures were much discussed. The dragons pricked up their ears. They were hungry, and these rumours were attractive.

"So knights are mythical!" said the younger and less experienced dragons. "We always thought so."

"At least they may be getting rare," thought the

older and wiser worms; "far and few and no longer to be feared."

There was one dragon who was deeply moved. Chrysophylax Dives was his name, for he was of ancient and imperial lineage, and very rich. He was cunning, inquisitive, greedy, well-armoured, but not over bold. But at any rate he was not in the least afraid of flies or insects of any sort or size; and he was mortally hungry.

So one winter's day, about a week before Christmas, Chrysophylax spread his wings and took off. He landed quietly in the middle of the night plump in the heart of the midland realm of Augustus Bonifacius rex et basileus. He did a deal of damage in a short while, smashing and burning, and devouring sheep, cattle, and horses.

This was in a part of the land a long way from Ham, but Garm got the fright of his life. He had gone off on a long expedition, and taking advantage of his master's favour he had ventured to spend a night or two away from home. He was following an engaging scent along the eaves of a wood, when he turned a corner and came suddenly upon a new and alarming smell; he ran indeed slap into the tail of Chrysophylax Dives, who had just landed. Never did a dog turn his own tail round and bolt home swifter than Garm. The dragon, hearing his yelp, turned and snorted; but Garm was already far out of range. He ran all the rest of the night, and arrived home about breakfast-time.

"Help! help! help!" he cried outside the back door.

Giles heard, and did not like the sound of it. It reminded him that unexpected things may happen, when all seems to be going well.

"Wife, let that dratted dog in," said he, "and take a stick to him!"

Garm came bundling into the kitchen with his eyes starting and his tongue hanging out. "Help!" he cried.

"Now what have you been a-doing this time?" said Giles, throwing a sausage at him.

"Nothing," panted Garm, too flustered to give heed to the sausage.

"Well, stop doing it, or I'll skin you," said the farmer.

"I've done no wrong. I didn't mean no harm," said the dog. "But I came on a dragon accidental-like, and it frightened me."

The farmer choked in his beer. "Dragon?" said he. "Drat you for a good-for-nothing nosey-parker! What d'you want to go and find a dragon for, at this time of the year, and me with my hands full? Where was it?"

"Oh! North over the hills and far away, beyond the Standing Stones and all," said the dog.

"Oh, away there!" said Giles, mighty relieved. "They're queer folk in those parts, I've heard tell, and aught might happen in their land. Let them get on with it! Don't come worriting me with such tales. Get out!"

Garm got out, and spread the news all over the village. He did not forget to mention that his master was not scared in the least. "Quite cool he was, and went on with his breakfast."

People chatted about it pleasantly at their doors. "How like old times!" they said. "Just as Christmas is coming, too. So seasonable. How pleased the King will be! He will be able to have Real Tail this Christmas."

But more news came in next day. The dragon, it appeared, was exceptionally large and ferocious He was doing terrible damage.

"What about the King's knights?" people began to say.

Others had already asked the same question. Indeed, messengers were now reaching the King from the villages most afflicted by Chrysophylax, and they said to him as loudly and as often as they dared: "Lord, what of your knights?"

But the knights did nothing; their knowledge of the dragon was still quite unofficial. So the King brought the matter to their notice, fully and formally, asking for necessary action at their early convenience. He was greatly displeased when he found that their convenience would not be early at all, and was indeed daily postponed.

Yet the excuses of the knights were undoubtedly sound. First of all, the Royal Cook had already made the Dragon's Tail for that Christmas, being a man who believed in getting things done in good time. It would not do at all to offend him by bringing in a real tail at the last minute. He was a very valuable servant.

"Never mind the Tail! Cut his head off and put an end to him!" cried the messengers from the villages most nearly affected.

But Christmas had arrived, and most unfortunately a grand tournament had been arranged for St. John's Day: knights of many realms had been invited and were coming to compete for a valuable prize. It was obviously unreasonable to spoil the chances of the Midland Knights by sending their best men off on a dragon-hunt before the tournament was over.

After that came the New Year Holiday.

But each night the dragon had moved; and each move had brought him nearer to Ham. On the night of New Year's Day people could see a blaze in the distance. The dragon had settled in a wood about ten miles away, and it was burning merrily. He was a hot dragon when he felt in the mood.

After that people began to look at Farmer Giles and whisper behind his back. It made him very uncomfortable; but he pretended not to notice it. The next day the dragon came several miles nearer. Then Farmer Giles himself began to talk loudly of the scandal of the King's knights.

"I should like to know what they do to earn their keep," said he.

'So should we!" said everyone in Ham.

But the miller added: "Some men still get knighthood by sheer merit, I am told. After all, our good Ægidius here is already a knight in a manner of speaking. Did not the King send him a red letter and a sword?"

"There's more to knighthood than a sword," said Giles. "There's dubbing and all that, or so I understand. Anyway I've my own business to attend to."

"Oh! but the King would do the dubbing, I don't doubt, if he were asked," said the miller. "Let us ask him, before it is too late!"

"Nay!" said Giles. "Dubbing is not for my sort. I am a farmer and proud of it: a plain honest man, and honest men fare ill at court, they say. It is more in your line, Master Miller."

The parson smiled: not at the farmer's retort, for Giles and the miller were always giving one another as good as they got, being bosom enemies, as the saying was in Ham. The parson had suddenly been struck with a notion that pleased him, but he said no more at that time. The miller was not so pleased, and he scowled.

"Plain certainly, and honest perhaps," said he. "But do you have to go to court and be a knight before you kill a dragon? Courage is all that is needed, as only yesterday I heard Master Ægidius declare. Surely he has as much courage as any knight?"

All the folk standing by shouted: "Of course not!" and "Yes indeed! Three cheers for the Hero of Ham!"

Then Farmer Giles went home feeling very uncomfortable. He was finding that a local reputation may require keeping up, and that may prove awkward. He kicked the dog, and hid the sword in a cupboard in the kitchen. Up till then it had hung over the fireplace.

The next day the dragon moved to the neighbouring village of Quercetum (Oakley in the vulgar tongue). He ate not only sheep and cows and one or two persons of tender age, but he ate the parson too. Rather rashly the parson had sought to dissuade him from his evil ways. Then there was a terrible commotion. All the people of Ham came up the hill, headed by their own parson; and they waited on Farmer Giles.

"We look to you!" they said; and they remained standing round and looking, until the farmer's face was redder than his beard.

"When are you going to start?" they asked.

"Well, I can't start today, and that's a fact," said he. "I've a lot on hand with my cowman sick and all. I'll see about it."

They went away; but in the evening it was rumoured that the dragon had moved even nearer, so they all came back.

"We look to you, Master Ægidius," they said.

"Well," said he, "it's very awkward for me just now. My mare has gone lame, and the lambing has started. I'll see about it as soon as may be."

So they went away once more, not without

some grumbling and whispering. The miller was
sniggering. The parson stayed behind, and could
not be got rid of. He invited himself to supper,
and made some pointed remarks. He even asked
what had become of the sword and insisted on
seeing it.

It was lying in a cupboard on a shelf hardly long
enough for it, and as soon as Farmer Giles brought
it out in a flash it leaped from the sheath, which
the farmer dropped as if it had been hot. The
parson sprang to his feet, upsetting his beer. He

picked the sword up carefully and tried to put it
back in the sheath; but it would not go so much as
a foot in, and it jumped clean out again, as soon
as he took his hand off the hilt.

"Dear me! This is very peculiar!" said the parson,

and he took a good look at both scabbard and blade. He was a lettered man, but the farmer could only spell out large uncials with difficulty, and was none too sure of the reading even of his own name. That is why he had never given any heed to the strange letters that could dimly be seen on sheath and sword. As for the King's armourer, he was so accustomed to runes, names, and other signs of power and significance upon swords and scabbards that he had not bothered his head about them; he thought them out of date, anyway.

But the parson looked long, and he frowned. He had expected to find some lettering on the sword or on the scabbard, and that was indeed the idea that had come to him the day before; but now he was surprised at what he saw, for letters and signs there were, to be sure, but he could not make head or tail of them.

"There is an inscription on this sheath, and some, ah, epigraphical signs are visible also upon the sword," he said.

"Indeed?" said Giles. "And what may that amount to?"

"The characters are archaic and the language barbaric," said the parson, to gain time. "A little closer inspection will be required." He begged the loan of the sword for the night, and the farmer let him have it with pleasure.

When the parson got home he took down many learned books from his shelves, and he sat up far into the night. Next morning it was discovered that the dragon had moved nearer still. All the people of Ham barred their doors and shuttered their windows; and those that had cellars went down into them and sat shivering in the candlelight.

But the parson stole out and went from door to door; and he told, to all who would listen through a crack or a keyhole, what he had discovered in his study.

"Our good Ægidius," he said, "by the King's grace is now the owner of Caudimordax, the famous sword that in popular romances is more vulgarly called Tailbiter."

Those that heard this name usually opened the door. They all knew the renown of Tailbiter, for that sword had belonged to Bellomarius, the greatest of all the dragon-slayers of the realm Some accounts made him the maternal great-great-grandfather of the King. The songs and tales of his deeds were many, and if forgotten at court, were still remembered in the villages.

"This sword," said the parson, "will not stay sheathed, if a dragon is within five miles; and without doubt in a brave man's hands no dragon can resist it."

Then people began to take heart again; and some unshuttered the windows and put their heads out. In the end the parson persuaded a few to come and join him; but only the miller was really willing. To see Giles in a real fix seemed to him worth the risk.

They went up the hill, not without anxious looks north across the river. There was no sign of the dragon. Probably he was asleep; he had been feeding very well all the Christmas-time.

The parson (and the miller) hammered on the farmer's door. There was no answer, so they hammered louder. At last Giles came out. His face was very red. He also had sat up far into the night, drinking a good deal of ale; and he had begun again as soon as he got up.

They all crowded round him, calling him Good

Ægidius, Bold Ahenobarbus, Great Julius, Staunch Agricola, Pride of Ham, Hero of the Countryside. And they spoke of Caudimordax, Tailbiter, The Sword that would not be Sheathed, Death or Victory, The Glory of the Yeomanry, Backbone of the Country, and the Good of one's Fellow Men, until the farmer's head was hopelessly confused.

"Now then! One at a time!" he said, when he got a chance. "What's all this, what's all this? It's my busy morning, you know."

So they let the parson explain the situation. Then the miller had the pleasure of seeing the farmer in as tight a fix as he could wish. But things did not turn out quite as the miller expected. For one thing Giles had drunk a deal of strong ale. For another he had a queer feeling of pride and encouragement when he learned that his sword was actually Tailbiter. He had been very fond of tales about Bellomarius when he was a boy, and before he had learned sense he had sometimes wished that he could have a marvellous and heroic sword of his own. So it came over him all of a sudden that he would take Tailbiter and go dragon-hunting. But he had been used to bargaining all his life, and he made one more effort to postpone the event.

"What!" said he. "Me go dragon-hunting? In my old leggings and waistcoat? Dragon-fights need some kind of armour, from all I've heard tell. There isn't any armour in this house, and that's a fact," said he.

That was a bit awkward, they all allowed; but they sent for the blacksmith. The blacksmith shook his head. He was a slow, gloomy man, vulgarly known as Sunny Sam, though his proper name was Fabricius Cunctator. He never whistled at his work, unless some disaster (such as frost in May) had duly occurred after he had foretold it. Since he was daily foretelling disasters of every kind, few happened that he had not foretold, and he was able to take the credit of them. It was his chief pleasure; so naturally he was reluctant to do anything to avert them. He shook his head again.

"I can't make armour out of naught," he said. "And it's not in my line. You'd best get the carpenter to make you a wooden shield. Not that it will help you much. He's a hot dragon."

Their faces fell; but the miller was not so easily to be turned from his plan of sending Giles to the dragon, if he would go; or of blowing the bubble of his local reputation, if he refused in the end. "What about ring-mail?" he said. "That would be a help; and it need not be very fine. It would be for business and not for showing off at court. What about your old leather jerkin, friend Ægidius? And there is a great pile of links and rings in the smithy. I don't suppose Master Fabricius himself knows what may be lying there."

"You don't know what you are talking about," said the smith, growing cheerful. "If it's real ring-mail you mean, then you can't have it. It needs the skill of the dwarfs, with every little ring fitting into four others and all. Even if I had the craft, I should be working for weeks. And we shall all be in our graves before them," said he, "or leastways in the dragon."

They all wrung their hands in dismay, and the blacksmith began to smile. But they were now so alarmed that they were unwilling to give up the miller's plan, and they turned to him for counsel.

"Well," said he, "I've heard tell that in the old days those that could not buy bright hauberks out of the Southlands would stitch steel rings on a leather shirt and be content with that. Let's see what can be done in that line!"

So Giles had to bring out his old jerkin, and the smith was hurried back to his smithy. There they rummaged in every corner and turned over the pile of old metal, as had not been done for many a year. At the bottom they found, all dull with rust, a whole heap of small rings, fallen from some forgotten coat, such as the miller had spoken of. Sam, more unwilling and gloomy as the task seemed more hopeful, was set to work on the spot, gathering and sorting and cleaning the rings; and when (as he was pleased to point out) these were clearly insufficient for one so broad of back and breast as Master Ægidius, they made him split up old chains and hammer the links into rings as fine as his skill could contrive.

They took the smaller rings of steel and stitched

them on to the breast of the jerkin, and the larger and clumsier rings they stitched on the back; and then, when still more rings were forthcoming, so hard was poor Sam driven, they took a pair of the farmer's breeches and stitched rings onto them. And up on a shelf in a dark nook of the smithy the miller found the old iron frame of a helmet, and he set the cobbler to work, covering it with leather as well as he could.

The work took them all the rest of that day, and

all the next day—which was Twelfthnight and
the eve of the Epiphany, but festivities were
neglected. Farmer Giles celebrated the occasion
with more ale than usual; but the dragon merci-
fully slept. For the moment he had forgotten all
about hunger or swords.

Early on the Epiphany they went up the hill,
carrying the strange result of their handiwork. Giles
was expecting them. He had now no excuses left

to offer; so he put on the mail jerkin and the
breeches. The miller sniggered. Then Giles put
on his top-boots and an old pair of spurs; and also
the leather-covered helmet. But at the last moment
he clapped an old felt hat over the helmet, and
over the mail coat he threw his big grey cloak.

"What is the purpose of that, Master?" they
asked.

"Well," said Giles, "if it is your notion to go dragon-hunting jingling and dingling like Canterbury Bells, it ain't mine. It don't seem sense to me to let a dragon know that you are coming along the road sooner than need be. And a helmet's a helmet, and a challenge to battle. Let the worm see only my old hat over the hedge, and maybe I'll get nearer before the trouble begins."

They had stitched on the rings so that they overlapped, each hanging loose over the one below, and jingle they certainly did. The cloak did something to stop the noise of them, but Giles cut a queer figure in his gear. They did not tell him so. They girded the belt round his waist with difficulty, and they hung the scabbard upon it; but he had to carry the sword, for it would no longer stay sheathed, unless held with main strength.

The farmer called for Garm. He was a just man according to his lights. "Dog," he said, "you are coming with me."

The dog howled. "Help! help!" he cried.

"Now stop it!" said Giles. "Or I'll give you worse than any dragon could. You know the smell of this worm, and maybe you'll prove useful for once."

Then Farmer Giles called for his grey mare. She gave him a queer look and sniffed at the spurs. But she let him get up; and then off they went, and none of them felt happy. They trotted through the village, and all the folk clapped and cheered, mostly from their windows. The farmer and his

mare put as good a face on it as they could; but Garm had no sense of shame and slunk along with his tail down.

They crossed the bridge over the river at the end of the village. When at last they were well out of sight, they slowed to a walk. Yet all too soon they passed out of the lands belonging to Farmer Giles and to other folk of Ham and came to parts that the dragon had visited. There were broken trees, burned hedges and blackened grass, and a nasty uncanny silence.

The sun was shining bright, and Farmer Giles began to wish that he dared shed a garment or two; and he wondered if he had not taken a pint too many. "A nice end to Christmas and all," he thought. "And I'll be lucky if it don't prove the end of me too." He mopped his face with a large handkerchief—green, not red; for red rags infuriate dragons, or so he had heard tell.

But he did not find the dragon. He rode down many lanes, wide and narrow, and over other farmers' deserted fields, and still he did not find the dragon. Garm was, of course, of no use at all. He kept just behind the mare and refused to use his nose.

They came at last to a winding road that had suffered little damage and seemed quiet and peaceful. After following it for half a mile Giles began to wonder whether he had not done his duty and all that his reputation required. He had made up his mind that he had looked long and far enough, and he was just thinking of turning back, and of his dinner, and of telling his friends that the dragon had seen him coming and simply flown away, when he turned a sharp corner.

There was the dragon, lying half across a broken hedge with his horrible head in the middle of the road. "Help!" said Garm and bolted. The grey mare sat down plump, and Farmer Giles went off backwards into a ditch. When he put his head out, there was the dragon wide awake looking at him.

"Good morning!" said the dragon. "You seem surprised."

"Good morning!" said Giles. "I am that."

"Excuse me," said the dragon. He had cocked a very suspicious ear when he caught the sound of rings jingling, as the farmer fell. "Excuse my asking, but were you looking for me, by any chance?"

"No, indeed!" said the farmer. "Who'd a' thought of seeing you here? I was just going for a ride."

He scrambled out of the ditch in a hurry and backed away towards the grey mare. She was now on her feet again and was nibbling some grass at the wayside, seeming quite unconcerned.

"Then we meet by good luck," said the dragon. "The pleasure is mine. Those are your holiday clothes, I suppose. A new fashion, perhaps?" Farmer Giles's felt hat had fallen off and his grey cloak had slipped open; but he brazened it out.

"Aye," said he, "brand-new. But I must be after that dog of mine. He's gone after rabbits, I fancy."

"I fancy not," said Chrysophylax, licking his lips (a sign of amusement). "He will get home a long time before you do, I expect. But pray proceed on your way, Master—let me see, I don't think I know your name?"

"Nor I yours," said Giles; "and we'll leave it at that."

"As you like," said Chrysophylax, licking his lips again, but pretending to close his eyes. He had a wicked heart (as dragons all have), but not a very bold one (as is not unusual). He preferred a meal that he did not have to fight for; but appetite had returned after a good long sleep. The parson of Oakley had been stringy, and it was years since he had tasted a large fat man. He had now made up his mind to try this easy meat, and he was only waiting until the old fool was off his guard.

But the old fool was not as foolish as he looked, and he kept his eye on the dragon, even while he was trying to mount. The mare, however, had other ideas, and she kicked and shied when Giles tried to get up. The dragon became impatient and made ready to spring.

"Excuse me!" said he. "Haven't you dropped something?"

An ancient trick, but it succeeded; for Giles had indeed dropped something. When he fell he had dropped Caudimordax (or vulgarly Tailbiter), and there it lay by the wayside. He stooped to pick it up; and the dragon sprang. But not as quick as Tailbiter. As soon as it was in the farmer's hand, it leaped forward with a flash, straight at the dragon's eyes.

"Hey!" said the dragon, and stopped very short. "What have you got there?"

"Only Tailbiter, that was given to me by the King," said Giles.

"My mistake!" said the dragon. "I beg your pardon." He lay and grovelled, and Farmer Giles began to feel more comfortable. "I don't think you have treated me fair."

"How not?" said Giles. "And anyway why should I?"

"You have concealed your honourable name and pretended that our meeting was by chance; yet you are plainly a knight of high lineage. It used, sir, to be the custom of knights to issue a challenge in such cases, after a proper exchange of titles and credentials."

"Maybe it used, and maybe it still is," said Giles, beginning to feel pleased with himself. A man who has a large and imperial dragon grovelling before him may be excused, if he feels somewhat uplifted. "But you are making more mistakes than one, old worm. I am no knight. I am Farmer Ægidius of Ham, I am; and I can't abide trespassers. I've shot giants with my blunderbuss before now, for doing less damage than you have. And I issued no challenge neither."

The dragon was disturbed. "Curse that giant for a liar!" he thought. "I have been sadly misled. And now what on earth does one do with a bold farmer and a sword so bright and aggressive?" He could recall no precedent for such a situation. "Chrysophylax is my name," said he, "Chrysophylax the Rich. What can I do for your honour?" he added ingratiatingly, with one eye on the sword, and hoping to escape battle.

"You can take yourself off, you horny old varmint," said Giles, also hoping to escape battle. "I only want to be shut of you. Go right away from here, and get back to your own dirty den!" He stepped towards Chrysophylax, waving his arms as if he was scaring crows.

That was quite enough for Tailbiter. It circled flashing in the air; then down it came, smiting the dragon on the joint of the right wing, a ringing blow that shocked him exceedingly. Of course Giles knew very little about the right methods of killing a dragon, or the sword might have landed in a tenderer spot; but Tailbiter did the best it could in inexperienced hands. It was quite enough for Chrysophylax—he could not use his wing for days.

Up he got and turned to fly, and found that he could not. The farmer sprang on the mare's back. The dragon began to run. So did the mare. The dragon galloped over a field puffing and blowing. So did the mare. The farmer bawled and shouted, as if he was watching a horse race; and all the while he waved Tailbiter. The faster the dragon ran the more bewildered he became; and all the while the grey mare put her best leg foremost and kept close behind him.

On they pounded down the lanes, and through the gaps in the fences, over many fields and across many brooks. The dragon was smoking and bellowing and losing all sense of direction. At last they came suddenly to the bridge of Ham, thundered over it, and came roaring down the village street. There Garm had the impudence to sneak out of an alley and join in the chase.

All the people were at their windows or on the roofs. Some laughed and some cheered; and some beat tins and pans and kettles; and others blew horns and pipes and whistles; and the parson had the church bells rung. Such a to-do and an on-going had not been heard in Ham for a hundred years.

Just outside the church the dragon gave up. He lay down in the middle of the road and gasped. Garm came and sniffed at his tail, but Chryso-phylax was past all shame.

"Good people, and gallant warrior," he panted, as Farmer Giles rode up, while the villagers gathered round (at a reasonable distance) with hayforks, poles, and pokers in their hands. "Good people, don't kill me! I am very rich, I will pay for all the damage I have done. I will pay for the funerals of all the people I have killed, especially the parson of Oakley; he shall have a noble ceno-taph—though he was rather lean. I will give you each a really good present, if you will only let me go home and fetch it."

"How much?" said the farmer.

"Well," said the dragon, calculating quickly. He noticed that the crowd was rather large. "Thirteen and eightpence each?"

"Nonsense!" said Giles. "Rubbish!" said the people. "Rot!" said the dog.

"Two golden guineas each, and children half price?" said the dragon.

"What about dogs?" said Garm. "Go on!" said the farmer. "We're listening."

"Ten pounds and a purse of silver for every soul, and gold collars for the dogs?" said Chrysophylax anxiously.

"Kill him!" shouted the people, getting impatient.

"A bag of gold for everybody, and diamonds for the ladies?" said Chrysophylax hurriedly.

"Now you're talking, but not good enough," said Farmer Giles. "You've left dogs out again," said Garm. "What size of bags?" said the men. "How many diamonds?" said their wives.

"Dear me! dear me!" said the dragon. "I shall be ruined."

"You deserve it," said Giles. "You can choose between being ruined and being killed where you lie." He brandished Tailbiter, and the dragon cowered. "Make up your mind!" the people cried, getting bolder and drawing nearer.

Chrysophylax blinked; but deep down inside him

he laughed: a silent quiver which they did not observe. Their bargaining had begun to amuse him. Evidently they expected to get something out of it. They knew very little of the ways of the wide and wicked world—indeed, there was no one now living in all the realm who had had any actual experience in dealing with dragons and their tricks. Chrysophylax was getting his breath back, and his wits as well. He licked his lips.

"Name your own price!" he said.

Then they all began to talk at once. Chrysophylax listened with interest. Only one voice disturbed him: that of the blacksmith.

"No good 'll come of it, mark my words," said he. "A worm won't return, say what you like. But no good will come of it, either way."

"You can stand out of the bargain, if that's your

mind," they said to him, and went on haggling, taking little further notice of the dragon.

Chrysophylax raised his head; but if he thought of springing on them, or of slipping off during the argument, he was disappointed. Farmer Giles was standing by, chewing a straw and considering; but Tailbiter was in his hand, and his eye was on the dragon.

"You lie where you be!" said he, "or you'll get what you deserve, gold or no gold."

The dragon lay flat. At last the parson was made spokesman and he stepped up beside Giles. "Vile Worm!" he said. "You must bring back to this spot all your ill-gotten wealth; and after recompensing those whom you have injured we will share it fairly among ourselves. Then, if you make a solemn vow never to disturb our land again, nor to stir up any other monster to trouble us, we will let you depart with both your head and your tail to your own home. And now you shall take such strong oaths to return (with your ransom) as even the conscience of a worm must hold binding."

Chrysophylax accepted, after a plausible show of hesitation. He even shed hot tears, lamenting his ruin, till there were steaming puddles in the road; but no one was moved by them. He swore many oaths, solemn and astonishing, that he would return with all his wealth on the feast of St. Hilarius and St. Felix. That gave him eight days, and far too short a time for the journey, as even those ignorant of geography might well have reflected. Nonetheless, they let him go, and escorted him as far as the bridge.

"To our next meeting!" he said, as he passed over the river. "I am sure we shall all look forward to it."

"We shall indeed," they said. They were, of course, very foolish. For though the oaths he had taken should have burdened his conscience with sorrow and a great fear of disaster, he had, alas! no conscience at all. And if this regrettable lack in one of imperial lineage was beyond the comprehension of the simple, at least the parson with his booklearning might have guessed it. Maybe he did. He was a grammarian, and could doubtless see further into the future than others.

The blacksmith shook his head as he went back to his smithy. "Ominous names," he said. "Hilarius and Felix! I don't like the sound of them."

The King, of course, quickly heard the news. It ran through the realm like fire and lost nothing in the telling. The King was deeply moved, for various reasons, not the least being financial; and he made up his mind to ride at once in person to Ham, where such strange things seemed to happen.

He arrived four days after the dragon's departure, coming over the bridge on his white horse, with many knights and trumpeters, and a large baggage-train. All the people had put on their best clothes and lined the street to welcome him. The cavalcade came to a halt in the open space before the church gate. Farmer Giles knelt before the King, when he was presented; but the King told him to rise, and actually patted him on the back. The knights pretended not to observe this familiarity.

The King ordered the whole village to assemble in Farmer Giles's large pasture beside the river; and when they were all gathered together (including Garm, who felt that he was concerned), Augustus Bonifacius rex et basileus was graciously pleased to address them.

He explained carefully that the wealth of the miscreant Chrysophylax all belonged to himself as

lord of the land. He passed rather lightly over his
claim to be considered suzerain of the mountain-
country (which was debatable); but "we make no
doubt in any case," said he, "that all the treasure
of this worm was stolen from our ancestors. Yet
we are, as all know, both just and generous, and
our good liege Ægidius shall be suitably rewarded;
nor shall any of our loyal subjects in this place go
without some token of our esteem, from the parson
to the youngest child. For we are well pleased with
Ham. Here at least a sturdy and uncorrupted folk
still retain the ancient courage of our race." The
knights were talking among themselves about the
new fashion in hats.

The people bowed and curtsied, and thanked
him humbly. But they wished now that they had
closed with the dragon's offer of ten pounds all
round, and kept the matter private. They knew
enough, at any rate, to feel sure that the King's
esteem would not rise to that. Garm noticed that
there was no mention of dogs. Farmer Giles was
the only one of them who was really content. He
felt sure of some reward, and was mighty glad
anyway to have come safely out of a nasty business
with his local reputation higher than ever.

The King did not go away. He pitched his pa-
vilions in Farmer Giles's field, and waited for
January the fourteenth, making as merry as he

could in a miserable village far from the capital. The royal retinue ate up nearly all the bread, butter, eggs, chickens, bacon and mutton, and drank up every drop of old ale there was in the place in the next three days. Then they began to grumble at short commons. But the King paid handsomely for everything (in tallies to be honoured later by the Exchequer, which he hoped would shortly be richly replenished); so the folk of Ham were well satisfied, not knowing the actual state of the Exchequer.

January the fourteenth came, the feast of Hilarius and of Felix, and everybody was up and about early. The knights put on their armour. The farmer put on his coat of home-made mail, and they smiled openly, until they caught the King's frown. The farmer also put on Tailbiter, and it went into its sheath as easy as butter, and stayed there. The parson looked hard at the sword, and nodded to himself. The blacksmith laughed.

Midday came. People were too anxious to eat much. The afternoon passed slowly. Still Tailbiter showed no sign of leaping from the scabbard. None of the watchers on the hill, nor any of the small boys who had climbed to the tops of tall trees, could see anything by air or by land that might herald the return of the dragon.

The blacksmith walked about whistling; but it was not until evening fell and the stars came out that the other folk of the village began to suspect that the dragon did not mean to come back at all. Still they recalled his many solemn and astonishing oaths and kept on hoping. When, however, midnight struck and the appointed day was over, their disappointment was deep. The blacksmith was delighted.

"I told you so," he said. But they were still not convinced.

"After all he was badly hurt," said some.

"We did not give him enough time," said others. "It is a powerful long way to the mountains, and he would have a lot to carry. Maybe he has had to get help."

But the next day passed and the next. Then they all gave up hope. The King was in a red rage. The victuals and drink had run out, and the knights were grumbling loudly. They wished to go back to the merriments of court. But the King wanted money.

He took leave of his loyal subjects, but he was short and sharp about it; and he cancelled half the tallies on the Exchequer. He was quite cold to Farmer Giles and dismissed him with a nod.

"You will hear from us later," he said, and rode off with his knights and his trumpeters.

The more hopeful and simple-minded thought that a message would soon come from the court to summon Master Ægidius to the King, to be knighted at the least. In a week the message came, but it was of different sort. It was written and signed in triplicate: one copy for Giles; one for the parson; and one to be nailed on the church door. Only the copy addressed to the parson was of any use, for the court-hand was peculiar and as dark to the folk of Ham as the Book-latin. But the parson rendered it into the vulgar tongue and read it from the pulpit. It was short and to the point (for a royal letter); the King was in a hurry.

"We Augustus B. A. A. P and M. rex et cetera make known that we have determined, for the safety of our realm and for the keeping of our honour, that the worm or dragon styling himself Chrysophylax the Rich shall be sought out and condignly punished for his misdemeanours, torts, felonies, and foul perjury. All the knights of our Royal Household are hereby commanded to arm and make ready to ride upon this quest, so soon as Master Ægidius A. J. Agricola shall arrive at this our court. Inasmuch as the said Ægidius has proved himself a trusty man and well able to deal with giants, dragons, and other enemies of the King's peace, now therefore we command him to ride forth at once, and to join the company of our knights with all speed."

People said this was a high honour and next-door to being dubbed. The miller was envious. "Friend Ægidius is rising in the world," said he. "I hope he will know us when he gets back."

"Maybe he never will," said the blacksmith.

"That's enough from you, old horse-face!" said the farmer, mighty put out. "Honour be blowed! If I get back even the miller's company will be welcome. Still, it is some comfort to think that I shall be missing you both for a bit." And with that he left them.

You cannot offer excuses to the King as you can to your neighbours; so lambs or no lambs, ploughing or none, milk or water, he had to get up on his grey mare and go. The parson saw him off.

"I hope you are taking some stout rope with you?" he said.

"What for?" said Giles. "To hang myself?"

"Nay! Take heart, Master Ægidius!" said the parson. "It seems to me that you have a luck that you can trust. But take also a long rope, for you may need it, unless my foresight deceives me. And now farewell, and return safely!"

"Aye! And come back and find all my house and land in a pickle. Blast dragons!" said Giles. Then, stuffing a great coil of rope in a bag by his saddle, he climbed up and rode off.

He did not take the dog, who had kept well out of sight all the morning. But when he was gone,

Garm slunk home and stayed there, and howled all the night, and was beaten for it, and went on howling.

"Help, ow help!" he cried. "I'll never see dear master again, and he was so terrible and splendid. I wish I had gone with him, I do."

"Shut up!" said the farmer's wife, "or you'll never live to see if he comes back or he don't."

The blacksmith heard the howls. "A bad omen," he said cheerfully.

Many days passed and no news came. "No news is bad news," he said, and burst into song.

When Farmer Giles got to court he was tired and dusty. But the knights, in polished mail and with shining helmets on their heads, were all standing by their horses. The King's summons and the inclusion of the farmer had annoyed them, and so they insisted on obeying orders literally, setting off the moment that Giles arrived. The poor farmer had barely time to swallow a sop in a draught of wine before he was off on the road again. The mare was offended. What she thought of the King was luckily unexpressed, as it was highly disloyal.

It was already late in the day. "Too late in the day to start a dragon-hunt," thought Giles. But they did not go far. The knights were in no hurry, once they had started. They rode along at their leisure,

in a straggling line, knights, esquires, servants, and ponies trussed with baggage; and Farmer Giles jogging behind on his tired mare.

When evening came, they halted and pitched their tents. No provision had been made for Farmer Giles and he had to borrow what he could. The mare was indignant, and she forswore her allegiance to the house of Augustus Bonifacius.

The next day they rode on, and all the day after. On the third day they descried in the distance the dim and inhospitable mountains. Before long they were in regions where the lordship of Augustus Bonifacius was not universally acknowledged. They rode then with more care and kept closer together.

On the fourth day they reached the Wild Hills and the borders of the dubious lands where legendary creatures were reputed to dwell. Suddenly one of those riding ahead came upon ominous footprints in the sand by a stream. They called for the farmer.

"What are these, Master Ægidius?" they said.

"Dragon-marks," said he.

"Lead on!" said they.

So now they rode west with Farmer Giles at their head, and all the rings were jingling on his leather coat. That mattered little; for all the knights were laughing and talking, and a minstrel rode with them singing a lay. Every now and again they took up the refrain of the song and sang it all together, very loud and strong. It was encouraging, for the song was good—it had been made long before in days when battles were more common than tournaments; but it was unwise. Their coming was now known to all the creatures of that land, and the dragons were cocking their ears in all the caves of the West. There was no longer any chance of their catching old Chrysophylax napping.

As luck (or the grey mare herself) would have

it, when at last they drew under the very shadow of the dark mountains, Farmer Giles's mare went lame. They had now begun to ride along steep and stony paths, climbing upwards with toil and ever-growing disquiet. Bit by bit she dropped back in the line, stumbling and limping and looking so patient and sad that at last Farmer Giles was obliged to get off and walk. Soon they found themselves right at the back among the pack-ponies; but no one took any notice of them. The knights were discussing points of precedence and etiquette, and their attention was distracted. Otherwise they would have observed that dragon-marks were now obvious and numerous.

They had come, indeed, to the places where Chrysophylax often roamed, or alighted after taking his daily exercise in the air. The lower hills, and the slopes on either side of the path, had a scorched and trampled look. There was little grass, and the twisted stumps of heather and gorse stood up black amid wide patches of ash and burned earth. The region had been a dragons' playground for many a year. A dark mountain-wall loomed up before them.

Farmer Giles was concerned about his mare; but he was glad of the excuse for no longer being so conspicuous. It had not pleased him to be riding at the head of such a cavalcade in these dreary and dubious places. A little later he was gladder still, and had reason to thank his fortune (and his mare). For just about midday—it being then the Feast of Candlemas, and the seventh day of their riding—Tailbiter leaped out of its sheath, and the dragon out of his cave.

Without warning or formality he swooped out to give battle. Down he came upon them with a rush and a roar. Far from his home he had not shown himself over bold, in spite of his ancient and imperial lineage. But now he was filled with a great wrath; for he was fighting at his own gate, as it were, and with all his treasure to defend. He came round a shoulder of the mountain like a ton of thunderbolts, with a noise like a gale and a gust of red lightning.

The argument concerning precedence stopped short. All the horses shied to one side or the other, and some of the knights fell off. The ponies and the baggage and the servants turned and ran at once. They had no doubt as to the order of precedence.

Suddenly there came a rush of smoke that smothered them all, and right in the midst of it the dragon crashed into the head of the line. Several of the knights were killed before they could even issue their formal challenge to battle, and several others were bowled over, horses and all. As for the remainder, their steeds took charge of them, and turned round and fled, carrying their masters off, whether they wished it or no. Most of them wished it indeed.

But the old grey mare did not budge. Maybe she was afraid of breaking her legs on the steep stony path. Maybe she felt too tired to run away. She knew in her bones that dragons on the wing are worse behind you than before you, and you need more speed than a race-horse for flight to be useful. Besides, she had seen this Chrysophylax before, and remembered chasing him over field and brook in her own country, till he lay down tame in the village high-street. Anyway she stuck her legs out wide, and she snorted. Farmer Giles went as pale as his face could manage, but he stayed by her side; for there seemed nothing else to do.

And so it was that the dragon, charging down the line, suddenly saw straight in front of him his old enemy with Tailbiter in his hand. It was the last thing he expected. He swerved aside like a great bat and collapsed on the hillside close to the road. Up came the grey mare, quite forgetting to walk lame. Farmer Giles, much encouraged, had scrambled hastily on her back.

"Excuse me," said he, "but were you looking for me, by any chance?"

"No indeed!" said Chrysophylax. "Who would have thought of seeing you here? I was just flying about."

"Then we meet by good luck," said Giles, "and the pleasure is mine; for I was looking for *you*. What's more, I have a bone to pick with you, several bones in a manner of speaking."

The dragon snorted. Farmer Giles put up his arm to ward off the hot gust, and with a flash Tailbiter swept forward, dangerously near the dragon's nose.

"Hey!" said he, and stopped snorting. He began to tremble and backed away, and all the fire in him was chilled. "You have not, I hope, come to kill me, good master?" he whined.

"Nay! nay!" said the farmer. "I said naught about killing." The grey mare sniffed.

"Then what, may I ask are you doing with all these knights?" said Chrysophylax. "Knights always kill dragons, if we don't kill them first."

"I'm doing nothing with them at all. They're naught to me," said Giles. "And anyway, they are all dead now or gone. What about what you said last Epiphany?"

133

"What about it?" said the dragon anxiously.

"You're nigh on a month late," said Giles, and payment is overdue. I've come to collect it. You should beg my pardon for all the bother I have been put to."

"I do indeed!" said he. "I wish you had not troubled to come."

"It'll be every bit of your treasure this time, and no market-tricks," said Giles, "or dead you'll be, and I shall hang your skin from our church steeple as a warning."

"It's cruel hard!" said the dragon.

"A bargain's a bargain," said Giles.

"Can't I keep just a ring or two, and a mite of gold, in consideration of cash payment?" said he

"Not a brass button!" said Giles. And so they kept on for a while, chaffering and arguing like

folk at a fair. Yet the end of it was as you might expect; for whatever else might be said, few had ever outlasted Farmer Giles at a bargaining.

The dragon had to walk all the way back to his cave, for Giles stuck to his side with Tailbiter held mighty close. There was a narrow path that wound up and round the mountain, and there was barely room for the two of them. The mare came just behind and she looked rather thoughtful.

It was five miles, if it was a step, and stiff going; and Giles trudged along, puffing and blowing, but never taking his eye off the worm. At last on the west side of the mountain they came to the mouth of the cave. It was large and black and forbidding, and its brazen doors swung on great pillars of iron. Plainly it had been a place of strength and pride in days long forgotten; for dragons do not build such works nor delve such mines, but dwell rather, when they may, in the tombs and treasuries of mighty men and giants of old. The doors of this deep house were set wide, and in their shadow they halted. So far Chrysophylax had had no chance to escape, but coming now to his own gate he sprang forward and prepared to plunge in.

Farmer Giles hit him with the flat of the sword. "Woa!" said he. "Before you go in, I've something to say to you. If you ain't outside again in quick time with something worth bringing, I shall come in after you and cut off your tail to begin with."

The mare sniffed. She could not imagine Farmer Giles going down alone into a dragon's den for any money on earth. But Chrysophylax was quite prepared to believe it, with Tailbiter looking so bright and sharp and all. And maybe he was right, and the mare, for all her wisdom, had not yet understood the change in her master. Farmer Giles was backing his luck, and after two encounters was beginning to fancy that no dragon could stand up to him.

Anyway, out came Chrysophylax again in mighty quick time, with twenty pounds (troy) of gold and silver, and a chest of rings and necklaces and other pretty stuff.

"There!" said he.

"Where?" said Giles. "That's not half enough, if that's what you mean. Nor half what you've got, I'll be bound."

"Of course not!" said the dragon, rather perturbed to find that the farmer's wits seemed to have become brighter since that day in the village. "Of course not! But I can't bring it all out at once."

"Nor at twice, I'll wager," said Giles. "In you go again, and out again double quick, or I'll give you a taste of Tailbiter!"

"No!" said the dragon, and in he popped and out again double quick. "There!" said he, putting down an enormous load of gold and two chests of diamonds.

"Now try again!" said the farmer, "And try harder!"

"It's hard, cruel hard," said the dragon, as he went back in again.

But by this time the grey mare was getting a bit anxious on her own account. "Who's going to carry all this heavy stuff home, I wonder?" thought she; and she gave such a long sad look at all the bags and the boxes that the farmer guessed her mind.

"Never you worry, lass!" said he. "We'll make the old worm do the carting."

"Mercy on us!" said the dragon, who overheard these words as he came out of the cave for the third time with the biggest load of all, and a mort of rich jewels like green and red fire. "Mercy on us! If I carry all this, it will be near the death of me, and a bag more I never could manage, not if you killed me for it."

"Then there is more still, is there?" said the farmer.

"Yes," said the dragon, "enough to keep me respectable." He spoke near the truth for a rare wonder, and wisely as it turned out. "If you will leave me what remains," said he very wily, "I'll be your friend for ever. And I will carry all this treasure back to your honour's own house and not to the King's. And I will help you to keep it, what is more," said he.

Then the farmer took out a toothpick with his left hand, and he thought very hard for a minute. Then "Done with you!" he said, showing a laudable discretion. A knight would have stood out for the whole hoard and got a curse laid upon it. And as likely as not, if Giles had driven the worm to despair, he would have turned and fought in the end, Tailbiter or no Tailbiter. In which case Giles, if not slain himself, would have been obliged to slaughter his transport and leave the best part of his gains in the mountains.

Well, that was the end of it. The farmer stuffed his pockets with jewels, just in case anything went wrong; and he gave the grey mare a small load to carry. All the rest he bound on the back of Chrysophylax in boxes and bags, till he looked like a royal pantechnicon. There was no chance of his flying, for his load was too great, and Giles had tied down his wings.

"Mighty handy this rope has turned out in the end!" he thought, and he remembered the parson with gratitude.

So off now the dragon trotted, puffing and blowing, with the mare at his tail, and the farmer holding out Caudimordax very bright and threatening. He dared try no tricks.

In spite of their burdens the mare and the dragon made better speed going back than the cavalcade had made coming. For Farmer Giles was in a hurry—not the least reason being that he had little food in his bags. Also he had no trust in Chrysophylax after his breaking of oaths so solemn and binding, and he wondered much how to get through a night without death or great loss. But before that night fell he ran again into luck; for they overtook half a dozen of the servants and ponies that had departed in haste and were now wandering at a loss in the Wild Hills. They scattered in fear and amazement, but Giles shouted after them.

"Hey, lads!" said he. "Come back! I have a job for you, and good wages while this packet lasts."

So they entered his service, being glad of a guide, and thinking that their wages might indeed come more regular now than had been usual. Then they rode on, seven men, six ponies, one mare, and a dragon; and Giles began to feel like a lord and stuck out his chest. They halted as seldom as they could. At night Farmer Giles roped the dragon to four pickets, one to each leg, with three men to watch him in turn. But the grey mare kept half an eye open, in case the men should try any tricks on their own account.

After three days they were back over the borders of their own country; and their arrival caused such wonder and uproar as had seldom been seen between the two seas before. In the first village that they stopped at food and drink was showered on them free, and half the young lads wanted to join in the procession. Giles chose out a dozen likely young fellows. He promised them good wages, and bought them such mounts as he could get. He was beginning to have ideas.

After resting a day he rode on again, with his new escort at his heels. They sang songs in his honour: rough and ready, but they sounded good in his ears. Some folk cheered and others laughed. It was a sight both merry and wonderful.

Soon Farmer Giles took a bend southwards, and steered towards his own home, and never went near the court of the King nor sent any message. But the news of the return of Master Ægidius spread like fire from the West; and there was great astonishment and confusion. For he came hard on the heels of a royal proclamation bidding all the towns and villages to go into mourning for the fall of the brave knights in the pass of the mountains.

Wherever Giles went the mourning was cast aside, and bells were set ringing, and people thronged by the wayside shouting and waving their caps and their scarves. But they booed the poor dragon, till he began bitterly to regret the bargain he had made. It was most humiliating for one of ancient and imperial lineage. When they got back to Ham all the dogs barked at him scornfully. All except Garm: he had eyes, ears, and nose only for his master. Indeed, he went quite off his head, and turned somersaults all along the street.

Ham, of course, gave the farmer a wonderful

welcome; but probably nothing pleased him more than finding the miller at a loss for a sneer and the blacksmith quite out of countenance.

"This is not the end of the affair, mark my words!" said he; but he could not think of anything worse to say and hung his head gloomily. Farmer Giles, with his six men and his dozen likely lads and the dragon and all, went on up the hill, and there they stayed quiet for a while. Only the parson was invited to the house.

The news soon reached the capital, and forgetting the official mourning, and their business as well, people gathered in the streets. There was much shouting and noise.

The King was in his great house, biting his nails and tugging his beard. Between grief and rage (and financial anxiety) his mood was so grim that no one dared speak to him. But at last the noise of the town came to his ears: it did not sound like mourning or weeping.

"What is all the noise about?" he demanded. "Tell the people to go indoors and mourn decently! It sounds more like a goose-fair."

"The dragon has come back, lord," they answered.

"What!" said the King. "Summon our knights, or what is left of them!"

"There is no need, lord," they answered. "With

Master Ægidius behind him the dragon is tame as tame. Or so we are informed. The news has not long come in, and reports are conflicting."

"Bless our Soul!" said the King, looking greatly relieved. "And to think that we ordered a Dirge to be sung for the fellow the day after tomorrow! Cancel it! Is there any sign of our treasure?"

"Reports say that there is a veritable mountain of it, lord," they answered.

"When will it arrive?" said the King eagerly. "A good man this Ægidius—send him in to us as soon as he comes!"

There was some hesitation in replying to this. At last someone took courage and said: "Your pardon, lord, but we hear that the farmer has turned aside towards his own home. But doubtless he will hasten here in suitable raiment at the earliest opportunity."

"Doubtless," said the King. "But confound his raiment! He had no business to go home without reporting. We are much displeased."

The earliest opportunity presented itself, and passed, and so did many later ones. In fact, Farmer Giles had been back for a good week or more, and still no word or news of him came to the court.

On the tenth day the King's rage exploded. "Send for the fellow!" he said; and they sent. It was a day's hard riding to Ham, each way.

"He will not come, lord!" said a trembling messenger two days later.

"Lightning of Heaven!" said the King. "Command him to come on Tuesday next, or he shall be cast into prison for life!"

"Your pardon, lord, but he still will not come," said a truly miserable messenger returning alone on the Tuesday.

"Ten Thousand Thunders!" said the King. "Take this fool to prison instead! Now send some men to fetch the churl in chains!" he bellowed to those that stood by.

"How many men?" they faltered. "There's a dragon, and . . . and Tailbiter, and——."

"And broomstales and fiddlesticks!" said the King. Then he ordered his white horse, and summoned his knights (or what was left of them) and a company of men-at-arms, and he rode off in fiery anger. All the people ran out of their houses in surprise.

But Farmer Giles had now become more than the Hero of the Countryside: he was the Darling of the Land; and folk did not cheer the knights and men-at-arms as they went by, though they still took off their hats to the King. As he drew nearer to Ham the looks grew more sullen; in some villages the people shut their doors and not a face could be seen.

Then the King changed from hot wrath to cold anger. He had a grim look as he rode up at last to the river beyond which lay Ham and the house of the farmer. He had a mind to burn the place down. But there was Farmer Giles on the bridge, sitting on the grey mare with Tailbiter in his hand. No one else was to be seen, except Garm, who was lying in the road.

"Good morning, lord!" said Giles, as cheerful as day, not waiting to be spoken to.

The King eyed him coldly. "Your manners are unfit for our presence," said he; "but that does not excuse you from coming when sent for."

"I had not thought of it, lord, and that's a fact," said Giles. "I had matters of my own to mind, and had wasted time enough on your errands."

"Ten Thousand Thunders!" cried the King in a hot rage again. "To the devil with you and your insolence! No reward will you get after this; and you will be lucky if you escape hanging. And hanged you shall be, unless you beg our pardon here and now, and give us back our sword."

"Eh?" said Giles. "I have got my reward, I reckon. Finding's keeping, and keeping's having, we say here. And I reckon Tailbiter is better with me than with your folk. But what are all these knights and men for, by any chance?" he asked. "If you've come on a visit, you'd be welcome with fewer. If you want to take me away, you'll need a lot more."

The King choked, and the knights went very red and looked down their noses. Some of the men-at-arms grinned, since the King's back was turned to them.

"Give me my sword!" shouted the King, finding his voice, but forgetting his plural.

"Give us your crown!" said Giles: a staggering remark, such as had never before been heard in all the days of the Middle Kingdom.

"Lightning of Heaven! Seize him and bind him!" cried the King, justly enraged beyond bearing. "What do you hang back for? Seize him or slay him!"

The men-at-arms strode forward.

"Help! help! help!" cried Garm.

Just at that moment the dragon got up from under the bridge. He had lain there concealed under the far bank, deep in the river. Now he let off a terrible steam, for he had drunk many gallons of water. At once there was a thick fog, and only the red eyes of the dragon to be seen in it.

"Go home, you fools!" he bellowed. "Or I will tear you to pieces. There are knights lying cold in the mountain-pass, and soon there will be more in the river. All the King's horses and all the King's men!" he roared.

Then he sprang forward and struck a claw into the King's white horse; and it galloped away like the ten thousand thunders that the King mentioned so often. The other horses followed as swiftly: some had met this dragon before and did not like the memory. The men-at-arms legged it as best they could in every direction save that of Ham.

The white horse was only scratched, and he was not allowed to go far. After a while the King brought him back. He was master of his own horse at any rate; and no one could say that he was afraid of any man or dragon on the face of the earth. The fog was gone when he got back, but so were all his knights and his men. Now things looked very different with the King all alone to talk to a stout farmer with Tailbiter and a dragon as well.

But talk did no good. Farmer Giles was obstinate. He would not yield, and he would not fight, though the King challenged him to single combat there and then.

"Nay, lord!" said he, laughing. "Go home and get cool! I don't want to hurt you; but you had best be off, or I won't be answerable for the worm. Good day!"

And that was the end of the Battle of the Bridge of Ham. Never a penny of all the treasure did the King get, nor any word of apology from Farmer Giles, who was beginning to think mighty well of himself. What is more, from that day the power of the Middle Kingdom came to an end in that neighbourhood. For many a mile round about men took Giles for their lord. Never a man could the King with all his titles get to ride against the rebel Ægidius; for he had become the Darling of the Land, and the matter of song; and it was impossible to suppress all the lays that celebrated his deeds. The favourite one dealt with the meeting on the bridge in a hundred mock-heroic couplets.

Chrysophylax remained long in Ham, much to the profit of Giles; for the man who has a tame dragon is naturally respected. He was housed in the tithe-barn, with the leave of the parson, and there he was guarded by the twelve likely lads. In this way arose the first of the titles of Giles: Dominus de Domito Serpente, which is in the vulgar Lord of the Tame Worm, or shortly of Tame. As such he was widely honoured; but he still paid a nominal tribute to the King: six oxtails and a pint of bitter, delivered on St. Matthias' Day, that being the date of the meeting on the bridge. Before long, however, he advanced the Lord to Earl, and the belt of the Earl of Tame was indeed of great length.

After some years he became Prince Julius Ægidius and the tribute ceased. For Giles, being fabu-

lously rich, had built himself a hall of great
magnificence, and gathered great strength of men-
at-arms. Very bright and gay they were, for their
gear was the best that money could buy. Each of
the twelve likely lads became a captain. Garm
had a gold collar, and while he lived roamed at
his will, a proud and happy dog, insufferable to
his fellows; for he expected all other dogs to
accord him the respect due to the terror and
splendour of his master. The grey mare passed to
her days' end in peace and gave no hint of her
reflections.

In the end Giles became a king, of course, the

King of the Little Kingdom. He was crowned in Ham in the name of Ægidius Draconarius; but he was more often known as Old Giles Worming. For the vulgar tongue came into fashion at his court, and none of his speeches were in the Book-latin. His wife made a queen of great size and majesty, and she kept a tight hand on the household accounts. There was no getting round Queen Agatha—at least it was a long walk.

Thus Giles became at length old and venerable and had a white beard down to his knees, and a very respectable court (in which merit was often rewarded), and an entirely new order of knighthood. These were the Wormwardens, and a dragon was their ensign; the twelve likely lads were the senior members.

It must be admitted that Giles owed his rise in a large measure to luck, though he showed some wits in the use of it. Both the luck and the wits remained with him to the end of his days, to the great benefit of his friends and his neighbours. He rewarded the parson very handsomely; and even the blacksmith and the miller had their bit. For Giles could afford to be generous. But after he became king he issued a strong law against unpleasant prophecy, and made milling a royal monopoly. The blacksmith changed to the trade of an undertaker; but the miller became an obsequious servant of the crown. The parson became a bishop, and set up his see in the church of Ham, which was suitably enlarged.

Now those who live still in the lands of the Little Kingdom will observe in this history the true explanation of the names that some of its towns and villages bear in our time. For the learned in such matters inform us that Ham, being made the chief town of the new realm, by a natural confusion between the Lord of Ham and the Lord of Tame, became known by the latter name, which it retains to this day; for Thame with an *h* is a folly without warrant. Whereas in memory of the dragon, upon whom their fame and fortune were founded, the Draconarii built themselves a great house, four miles north-west of Tame, upon the spot where Giles and Chrysophylax first made acquaintance. That place became known throughout the kingdom as Aula Draconaria, or in the vulgar Worminghall, after the king's name and his standard.

The face of the land has changed since that time, and kingdoms have come and gone; woods have fallen, and rivers have shifted, and only the hills remain, and they are worn down by the rain and the wind. But still that name endures; though men now call it Wunnle (or so I am told); for villages have fallen from their pride. But in the days of which this tale speaks Worminghall it was,

and a Royal Seat, and the dragon-standard flew
above the trees; and all things went well
there and merrily, while Tailbiter
was above ground.

Envoy

Chrysophylax begged often for his liberty; and he proved expensive to feed, since he continued to grow, as dragons will, like trees, as long as there is life in them. So it came to pass, after some years, when Giles felt himself securely established, that he let the poor worm go back home. They parted with many expressions of mutual esteem, and a pact of non-aggression upon either side. In his bad heart of hearts the dragon felt as kindly disposed towards Giles as a dragon can feel towards anyone. After all there was Tailbiter: his life might easily have been taken, and all his hoard too. As it was, he still had a mort of treasure at home in his cave (as indeed Giles suspected).

He flew back to the mountains, slowly and laboriously, for his wings were clumsy with long disuse, and his size and his armour were greatly increased. Arriving home, he at once routed out a young dragon who had had the temerity to take up residence in his cave while Chrysophylax was away. It is said that the noise of the battle was heard throughout Venedotia. When, with great satisfaction, he had devoured his defeated opponent, he felt better, and the scars of his humiliation were assuaged, and he slept for a long while.

But at last, waking suddenly, he set off in search of that tallest and stupidest of the giants, who had started all the trouble one summer's night long before. He gave him a piece of his mind, and the poor fellow was very much crushed.

"A blunderbuss, was it?" said he, scratching his head. "I thought it was horseflies!"

Finis

or in the vulgar

THE END